4/12

# THE LEGEND OF SLEEPY HOLLOW

Adapted and Illustrated by
## Jeff Zornow

Based upon the works of
## Washington Irving

magic Wagon

Published by Magic Wagon, a division of the ABDO Publishing Group, 8000 West
78th Street, Edina, Minnesota 55439. Copyright © 2008 by Abdo Consulting
Group, Inc. International copyrights reserved in all countries. All rights reserved.
No part of this book may be reproduced in any form without written permission
from the publisher. Graphic Planet™ is a trademark and logo of Magic Wagon.


Printed in the United States of America, North Mankato, Minnesota.

Based upon the works of Washington Irving
Written & Illustrated by Jeff Zornow
Colored & Lettered by Lynx Studios
Edited & Directed by Chazz DeMoss
Cover Design by Neil Klinepier

J-GN

GRAPHIC PLANET

402-9503

*Library of Congress Cataloging-in-Publication Data*

Zornow, Jeff.
  The legend of Sleepy Hollow / adapted by Jeff Zornow ; based upon the works
of Washington Irving.
     p. cm. -- (Graphic horror)
  ISBN 978-1-60270-060-4
  1. Graphic novels. I. Irving, Washington, 1783-1859. Legend of Sleepy Hollow.
II. Title.
  PN6727.Z67L44 2007
  741.5'973--dc22

                                        2007009615

012008
062010

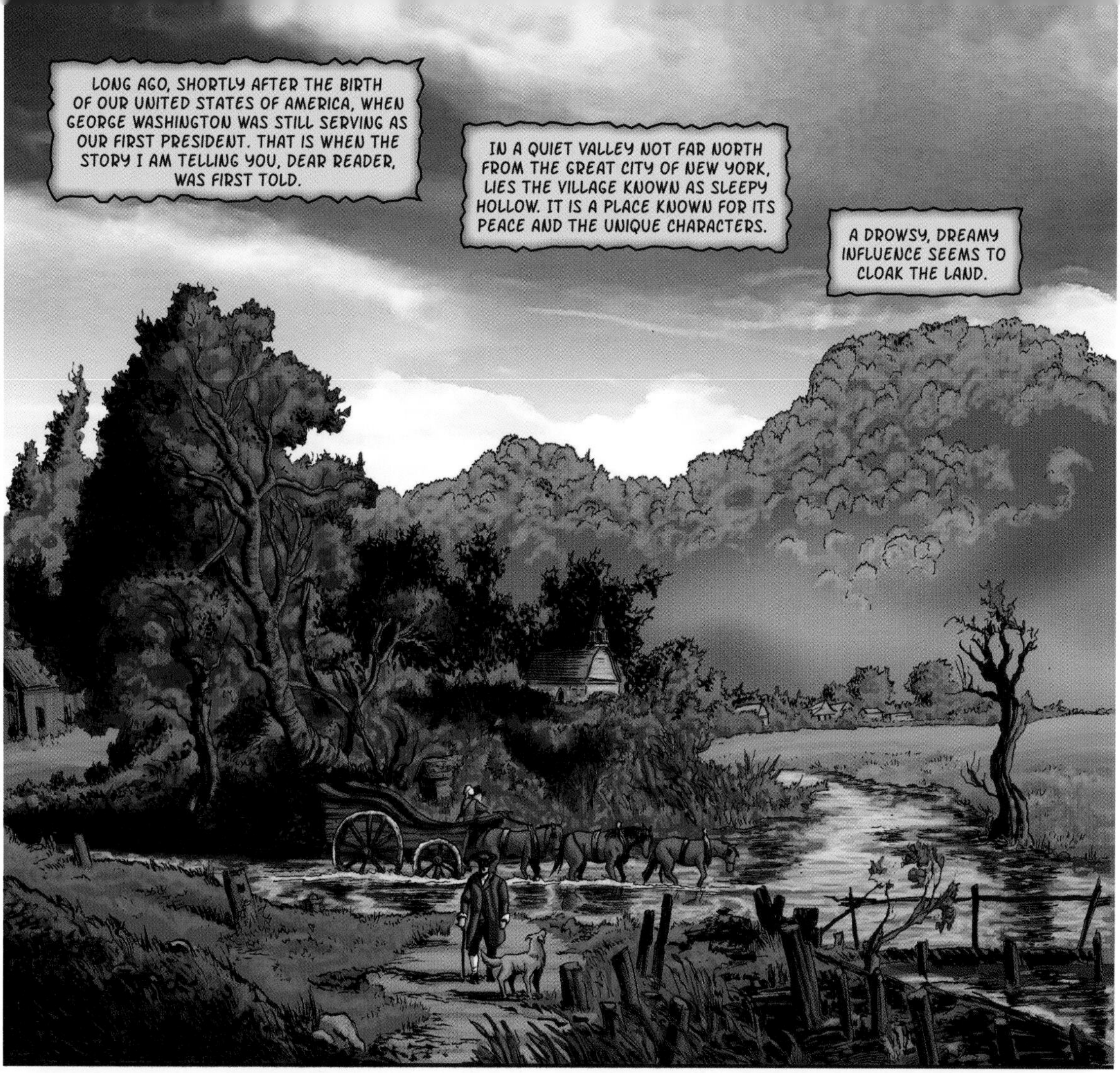
LONG AGO, SHORTLY AFTER THE BIRTH OF OUR UNITED STATES OF AMERICA, WHEN GEORGE WASHINGTON WAS STILL SERVING AS OUR FIRST PRESIDENT. THAT IS WHEN THE STORY I AM TELLING YOU, DEAR READER, WAS FIRST TOLD.
IN A QUIET VALLEY NOT FAR NORTH FROM THE GREAT CITY OF NEW YORK, LIES THE VILLAGE KNOWN AS SLEEPY HOLLOW. IT IS A PLACE KNOWN FOR ITS PEACE AND THE UNIQUE CHARACTERS.
A DROWSY, DREAMY INFLUENCE SEEMS TO CLOAK THE LAND.

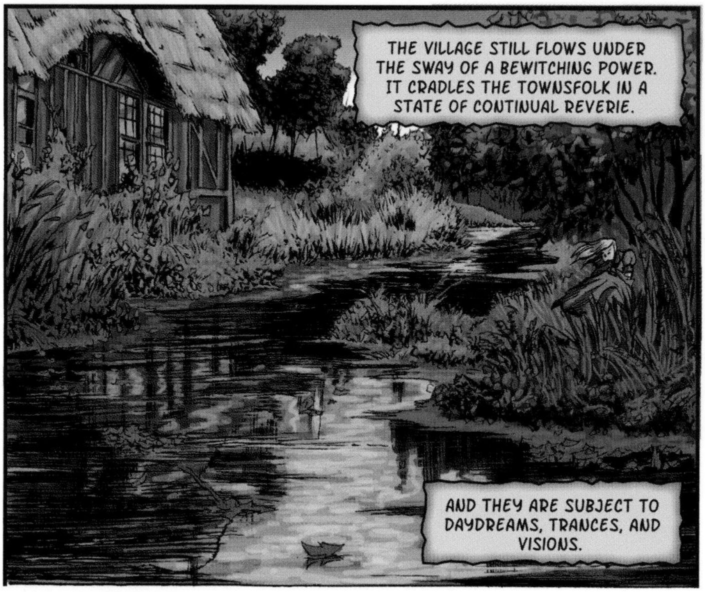
THE VILLAGE STILL FLOWS UNDER THE SWAY OF A BEWITCHING POWER. IT CRADLES THE TOWNSFOLK IN A STATE OF CONTINUAL REVERIE.
AND THEY ARE SUBJECT TO DAYDREAMS, TRANCES, AND VISIONS.

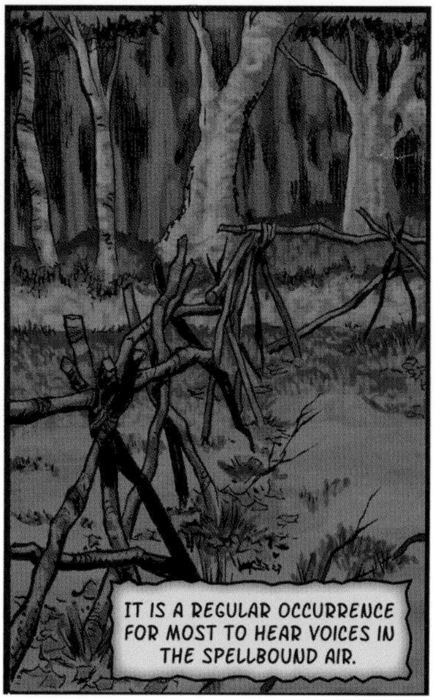
IT IS A REGULAR OCCURRENCE FOR MOST TO HEAR VOICES IN THE SPELLBOUND AIR.

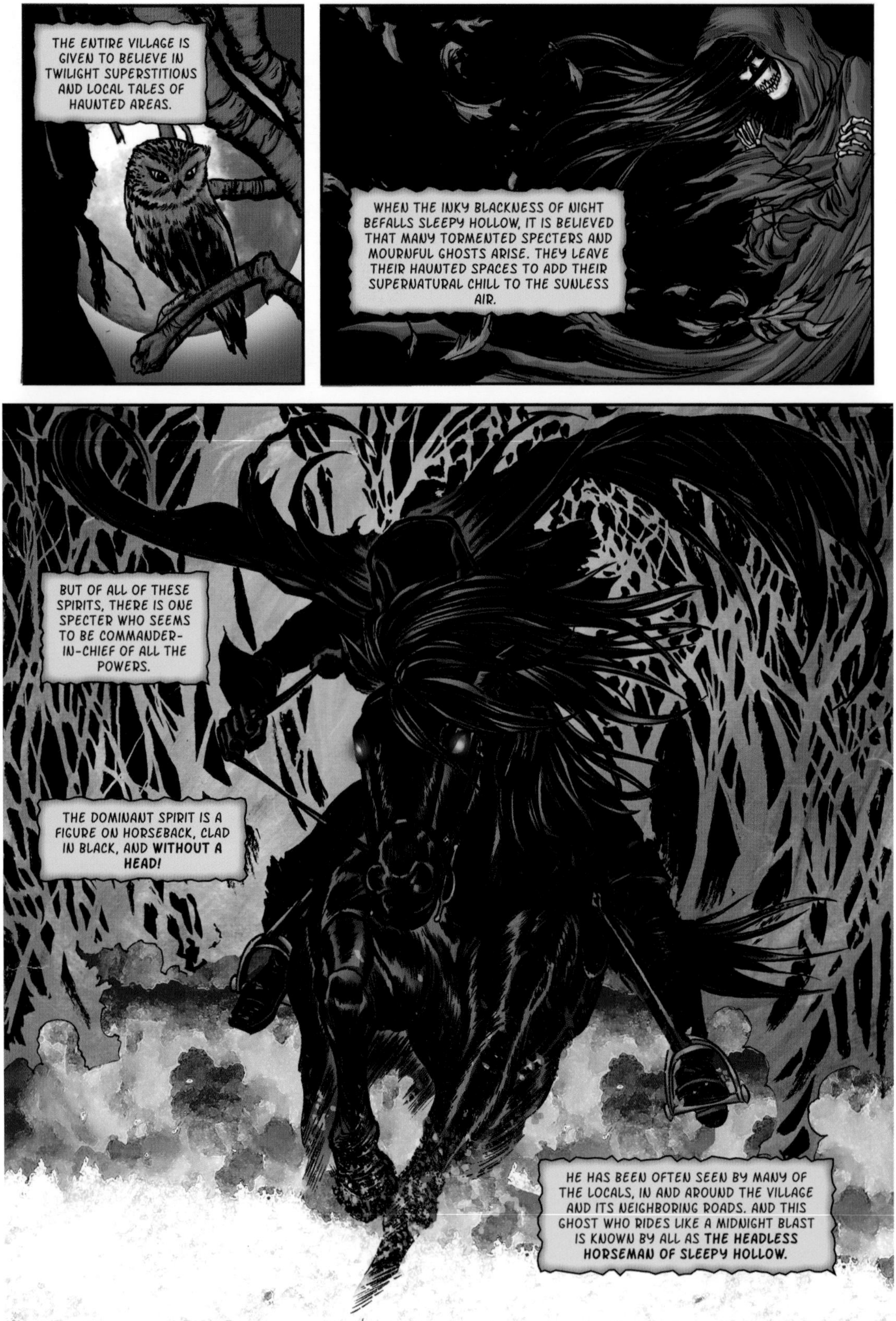
THE ENTIRE VILLAGE IS GIVEN TO BELIEVE IN TWILIGHT SUPERSTITIONS AND LOCAL TALES OF HAUNTED AREAS.
WHEN THE INKY BLACKNESS OF NIGHT BEFALLS SLEEPY HOLLOW, IT IS BELIEVED THAT MANY TORMENTED SPECTERS AND MOURNFUL GHOSTS ARISE. THEY LEAVE THEIR HAUNTED SPACES TO ADD THEIR SUPERNATURAL CHILL TO THE SUNLESS AIR.
BUT OF ALL OF THESE SPIRITS, THERE IS ONE SPECTER WHO SEEMS TO BE COMMANDER-IN-CHIEF OF ALL THE POWERS.
THE DOMINANT SPIRIT IS A FIGURE ON HORSEBACK, CLAD IN BLACK, AND **WITHOUT A HEAD!**
HE HAS BEEN OFTEN SEEN BY MANY OF THE LOCALS, IN AND AROUND THE VILLAGE AND ITS NEIGHBORING ROADS. AND THIS GHOST WHO RIDES LIKE A MIDNIGHT BLAST IS KNOWN BY ALL AS **THE HEADLESS HORSEMAN OF SLEEPY HOLLOW.**

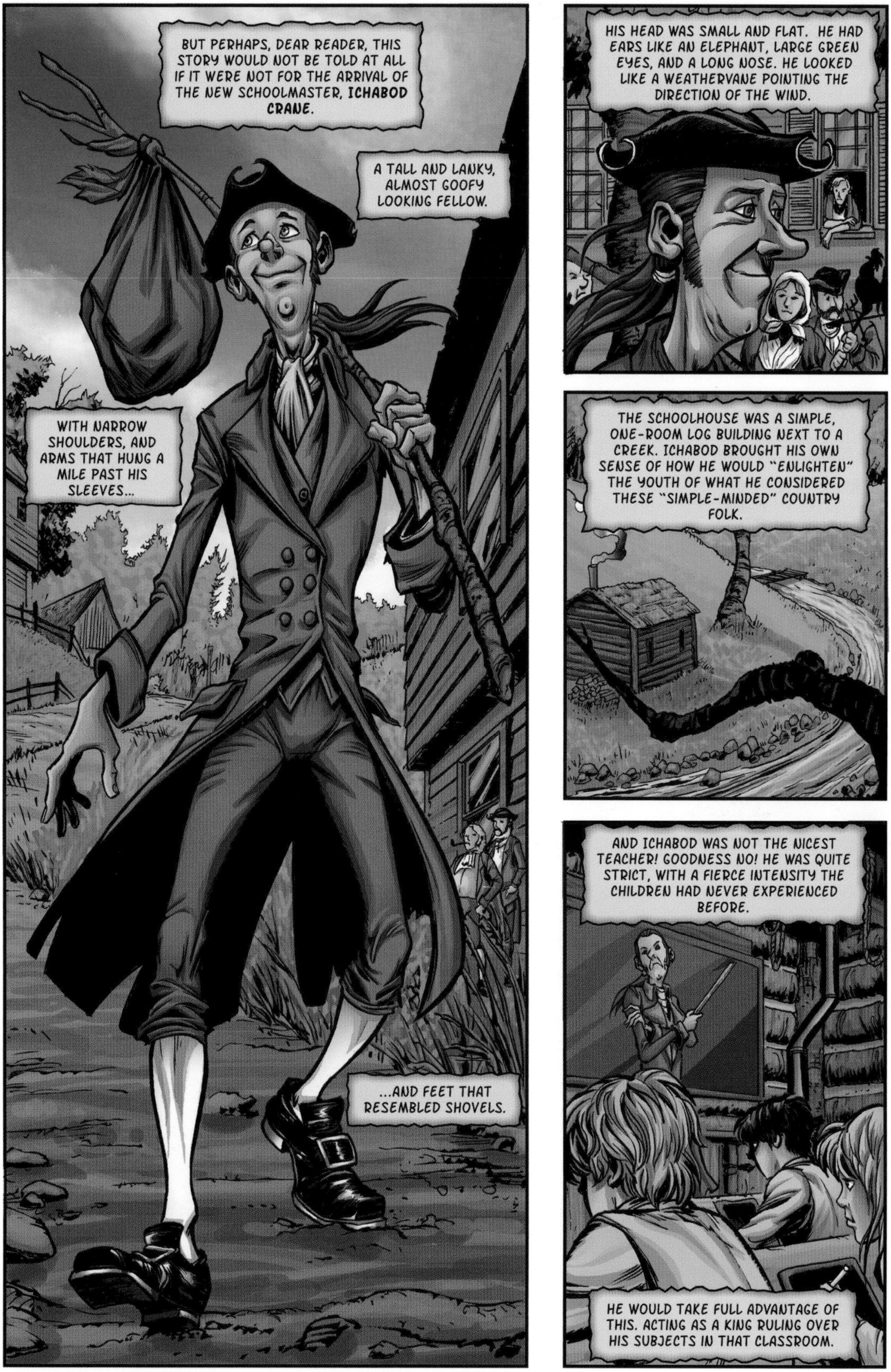
BUT PERHAPS, DEAR READER, THIS STORY WOULD NOT BE TOLD AT ALL IF IT WERE NOT FOR THE ARRIVAL OF THE NEW SCHOOLMASTER, **ICHABOD CRANE**.
A TALL AND LANKY, ALMOST GOOFY LOOKING FELLOW.
WITH NARROW SHOULDERS, AND ARMS THAT HUNG A MILE PAST HIS SLEEVES...
...AND FEET THAT RESEMBLED SHOVELS.
HIS HEAD WAS SMALL AND FLAT. HE HAD EARS LIKE AN ELEPHANT, LARGE GREEN EYES, AND A LONG NOSE. HE LOOKED LIKE A WEATHERVANE POINTING THE DIRECTION OF THE WIND.
THE SCHOOLHOUSE WAS A SIMPLE, ONE-ROOM LOG BUILDING NEXT TO A CREEK. ICHABOD BROUGHT HIS OWN SENSE OF HOW HE WOULD "ENLIGHTEN" THE YOUTH OF WHAT HE CONSIDERED THESE "SIMPLE-MINDED" COUNTRY FOLK.
AND ICHABOD WAS NOT THE NICEST TEACHER! GOODNESS NO! HE WAS QUITE STRICT, WITH A FIERCE INTENSITY THE CHILDREN HAD NEVER EXPERIENCED BEFORE.
HE WOULD TAKE FULL ADVANTAGE OF THIS. ACTING AS A KING RULING OVER HIS SUBJECTS IN THAT CLASSROOM.

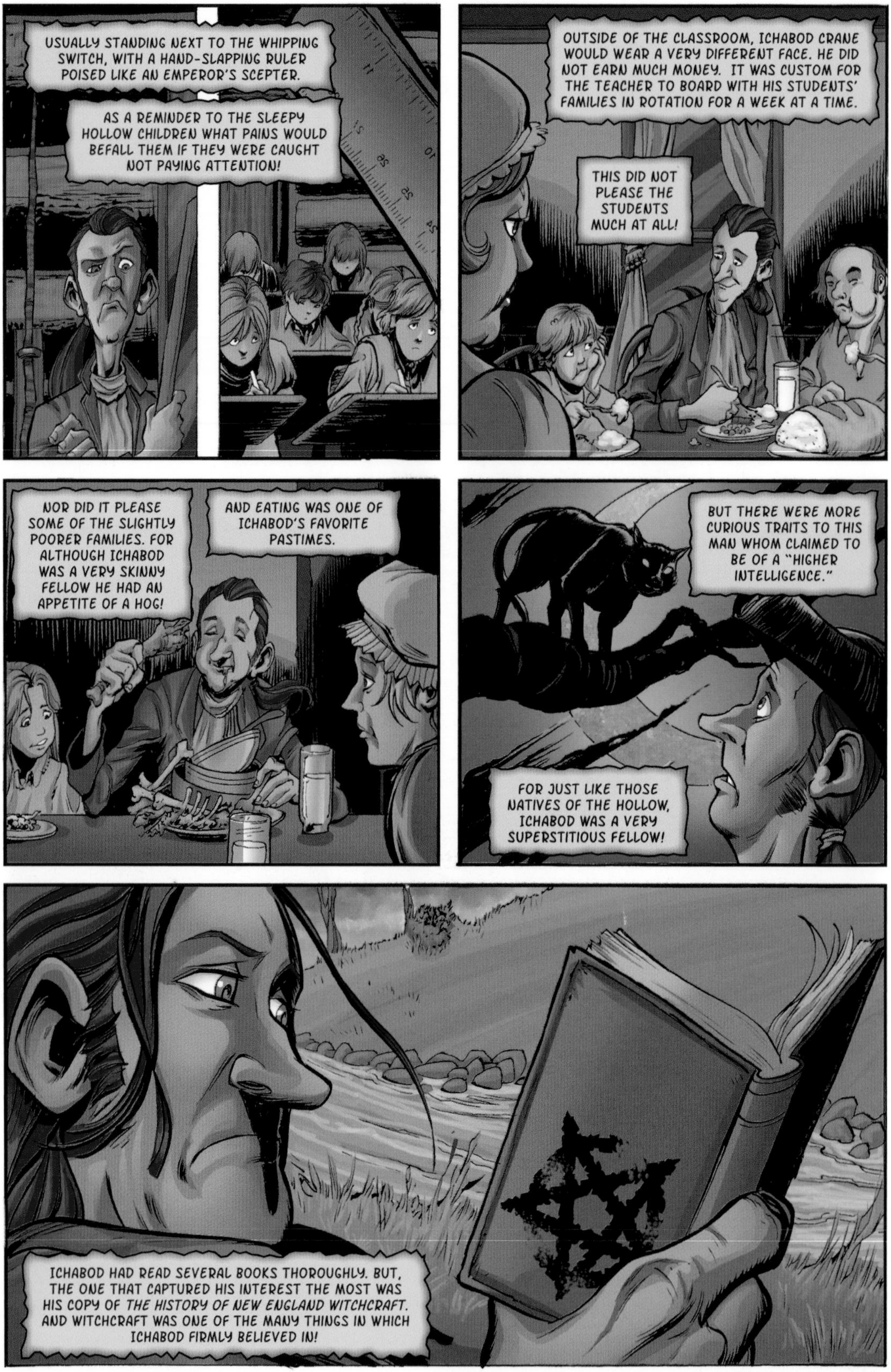
USUALLY STANDING NEXT TO THE WHIPPING SWITCH, WITH A HAND-SLAPPING RULER POISED LIKE AN EMPEROR'S SCEPTER.
AS A REMINDER TO THE SLEEPY HOLLOW CHILDREN WHAT PAINS WOULD BEFALL THEM IF THEY WERE CAUGHT NOT PAYING ATTENTION!
OUTSIDE OF THE CLASSROOM, ICHABOD CRANE WOULD WEAR A VERY DIFFERENT FACE. HE DID NOT EARN MUCH MONEY. IT WAS CUSTOM FOR THE TEACHER TO BOARD WITH HIS STUDENTS' FAMILIES IN ROTATION FOR A WEEK AT A TIME.
THIS DID NOT PLEASE THE STUDENTS MUCH AT ALL!
NOR DID IT PLEASE SOME OF THE SLIGHTLY POORER FAMILIES. FOR ALTHOUGH ICHABOD WAS A VERY SKINNY FELLOW HE HAD AN APPETITE OF A HOG!
AND EATING WAS ONE OF ICHABOD'S FAVORITE PASTIMES.
BUT THERE WERE MORE CURIOUS TRAITS TO THIS MAN WHOM CLAIMED TO BE OF A "HIGHER INTELLIGENCE."
FOR JUST LIKE THOSE NATIVES OF THE HOLLOW, ICHABOD WAS A VERY SUPERSTITIOUS FELLOW!
ICHABOD HAD READ SEVERAL BOOKS THOROUGHLY. BUT, THE ONE THAT CAPTURED HIS INTEREST THE MOST WAS HIS COPY OF *THE HISTORY OF NEW ENGLAND WITCHCRAFT*. AND WITCHCRAFT WAS ONE OF THE MANY THINGS IN WHICH ICHABOD FIRMLY BELIEVED IN!

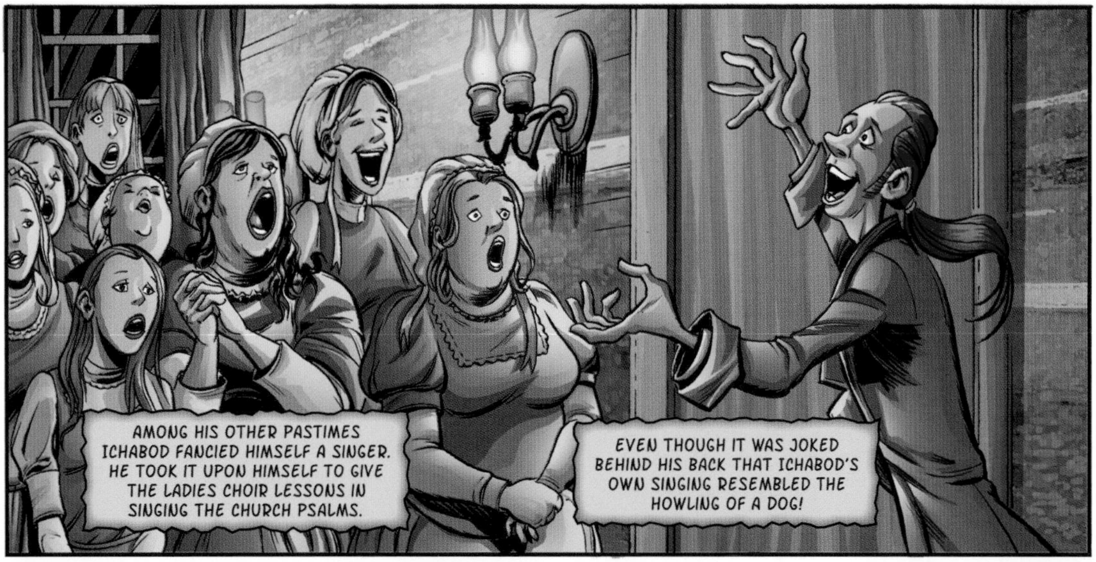
AMONG HIS OTHER PASTIMES ICHABOD FANCIED HIMSELF A SINGER. HE TOOK IT UPON HIMSELF TO GIVE THE LADIES CHOIR LESSONS IN SINGING THE CHURCH PSALMS.
EVEN THOUGH IT WAS JOKED BEHIND HIS BACK THAT ICHABOD'S OWN SINGING RESEMBLED THE HOWLING OF A DOG!

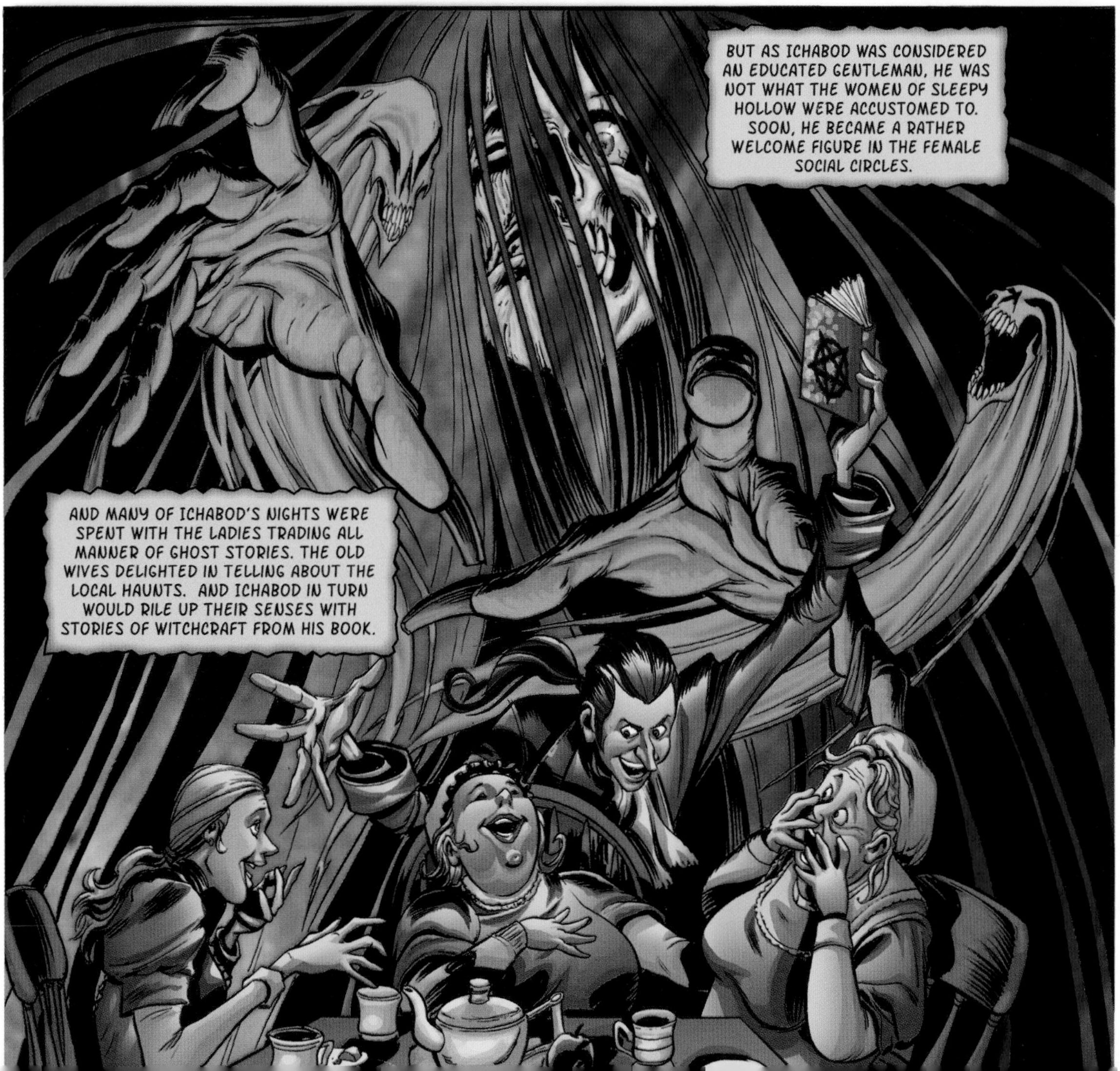
BUT AS ICHABOD WAS CONSIDERED AN EDUCATED GENTLEMAN, HE WAS NOT WHAT THE WOMEN OF SLEEPY HOLLOW WERE ACCUSTOMED TO. SOON, HE BECAME A RATHER WELCOME FIGURE IN THE FEMALE SOCIAL CIRCLES.
AND MANY OF ICHABOD'S NIGHTS WERE SPENT WITH THE LADIES TRADING ALL MANNER OF GHOST STORIES. THE OLD WIVES DELIGHTED IN TELLING ABOUT THE LOCAL HAUNTS. AND ICHABOD IN TURN WOULD RILE UP THEIR SENSES WITH STORIES OF WITCHCRAFT FROM HIS BOOK.

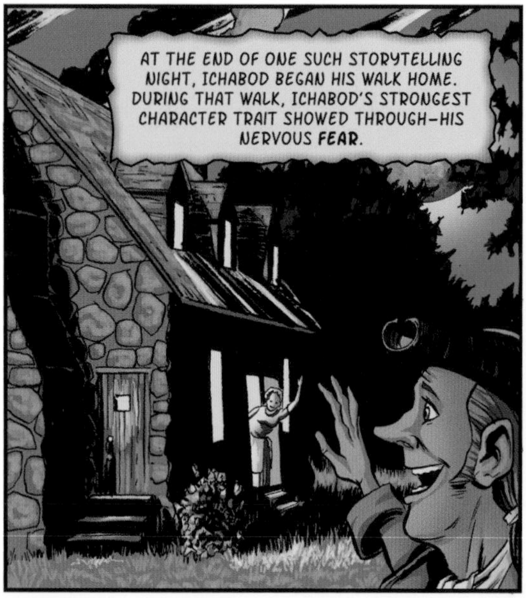
AT THE END OF ONE SUCH STORYTELLING NIGHT, ICHABOD BEGAN HIS WALK HOME. DURING THAT WALK, ICHABOD'S STRONGEST CHARACTER TRAIT SHOWED THROUGH–HIS NERVOUS FEAR.

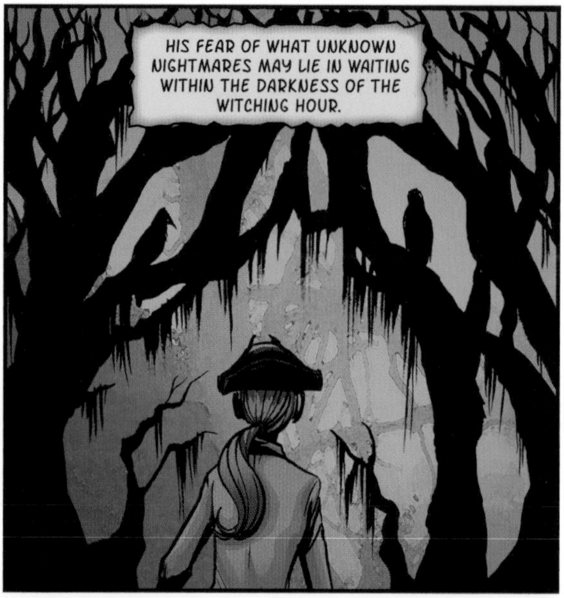
HIS FEAR OF WHAT UNKNOWN NIGHTMARES MAY LIE IN WAITING WITHIN THE DARKNESS OF THE WITCHING HOUR.

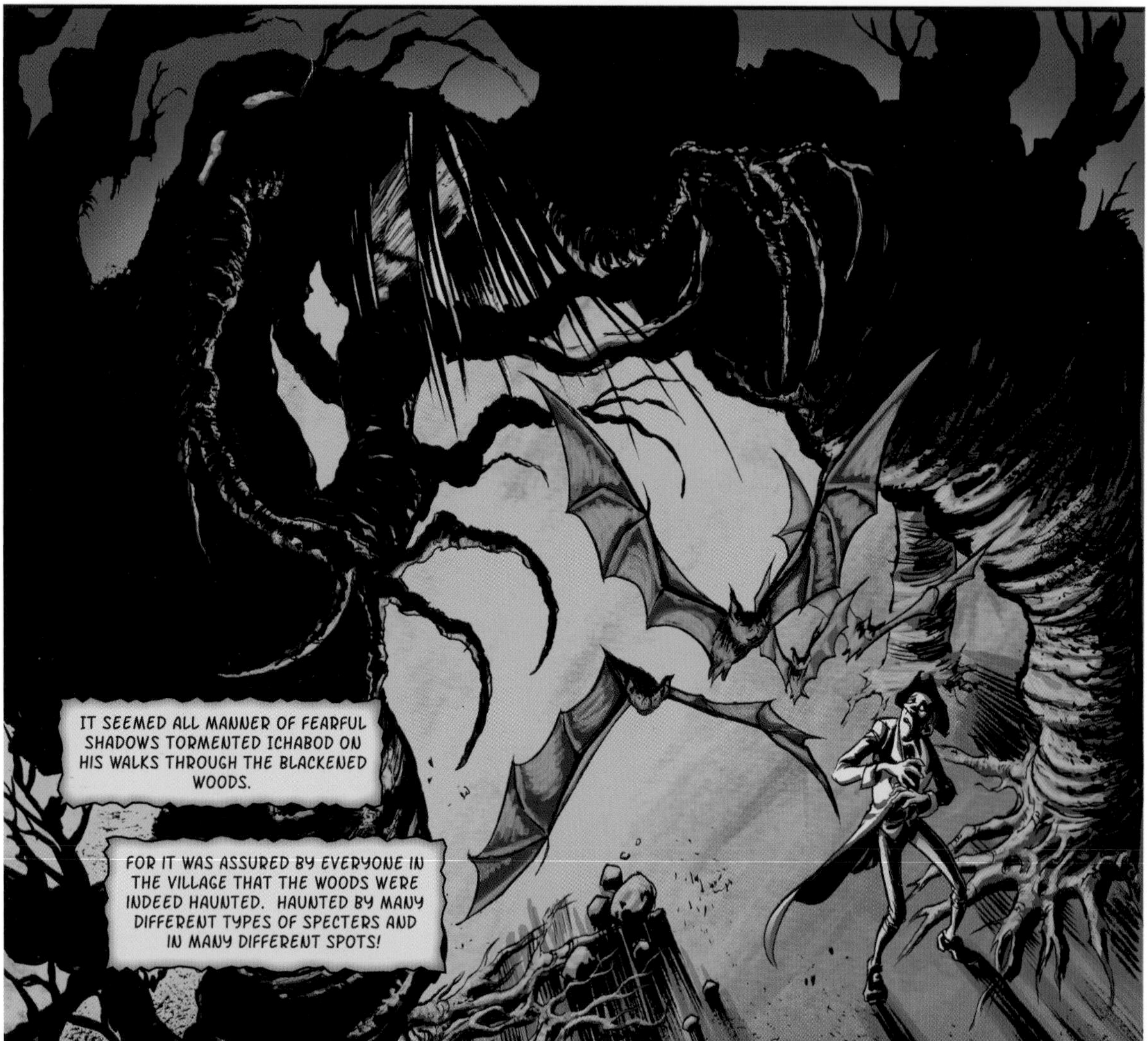
IT SEEMED ALL MANNER OF FEARFUL SHADOWS TORMENTED ICHABOD ON HIS WALKS THROUGH THE BLACKENED WOODS.
FOR IT WAS ASSURED BY EVERYONE IN THE VILLAGE THAT THE WOODS WERE INDEED HAUNTED. HAUNTED BY MANY DIFFERENT TYPES OF SPECTERS AND IN MANY DIFFERENT SPOTS!

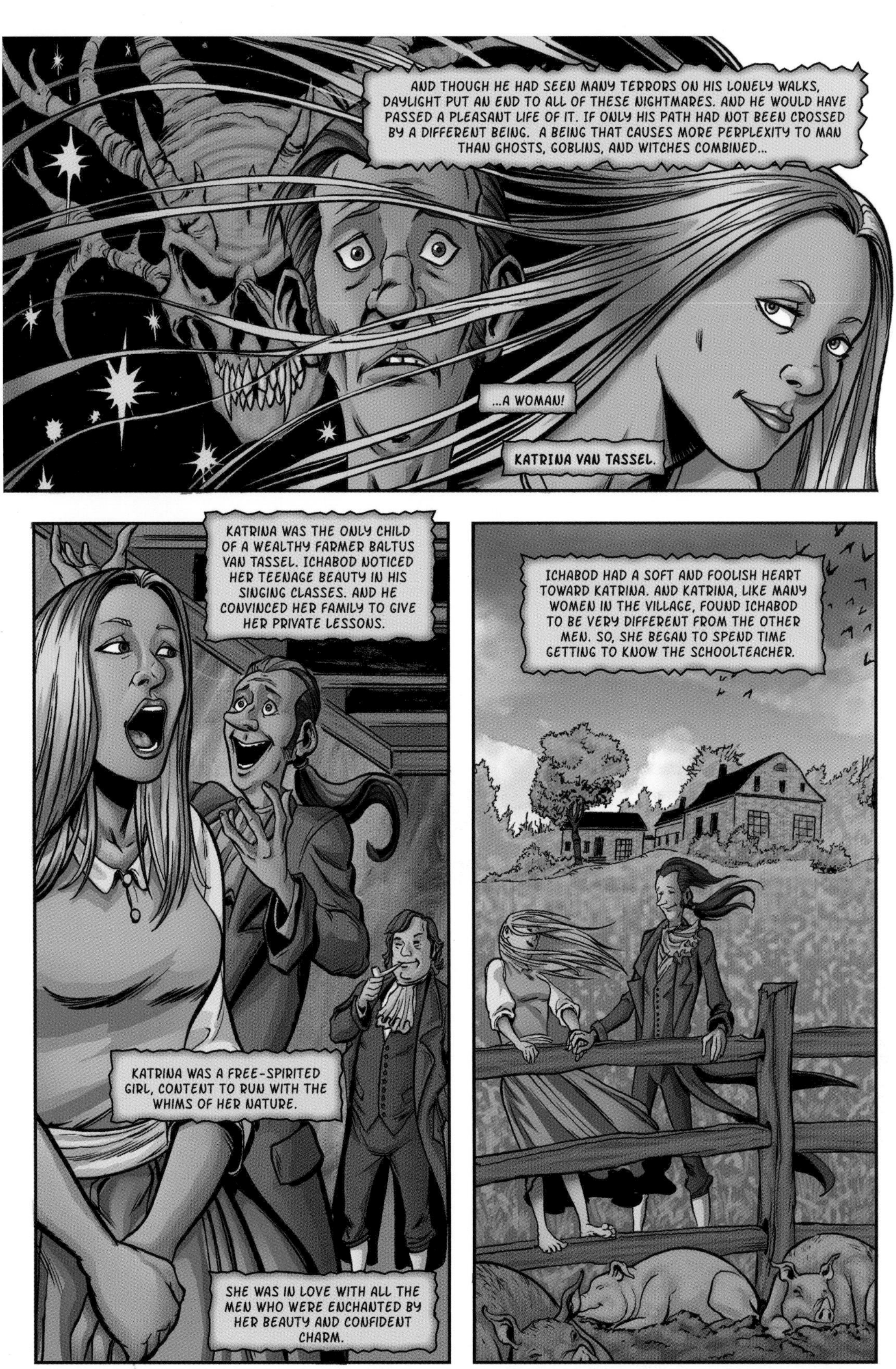
AND THOUGH HE HAD SEEN MANY TERRORS ON HIS LONELY WALKS, DAYLIGHT PUT AN END TO ALL OF THESE NIGHTMARES. AND HE WOULD HAVE PASSED A PLEASANT LIFE OF IT. IF ONLY HIS PATH HAD NOT BEEN CROSSED BY A DIFFERENT BEING. A BEING THAT CAUSES MORE PERPLEXITY TO MAN THAN GHOSTS, GOBLINS, AND WITCHES COMBINED...
...A WOMAN!
KATRINA VAN TASSEL.
KATRINA WAS THE ONLY CHILD OF A WEALTHY FARMER BALTUS VAN TASSEL. ICHABOD NOTICED HER TEENAGE BEAUTY IN HIS SINGING CLASSES. AND HE CONVINCED HER FAMILY TO GIVE HER PRIVATE LESSONS.
KATRINA WAS A FREE-SPIRITED GIRL, CONTENT TO RUN WITH THE WHIMS OF HER NATURE.
SHE WAS IN LOVE WITH ALL THE MEN WHO WERE ENCHANTED BY HER BEAUTY AND CONFIDENT CHARM.
ICHABOD HAD A SOFT AND FOOLISH HEART TOWARD KATRINA. AND KATRINA, LIKE MANY WOMEN IN THE VILLAGE, FOUND ICHABOD TO BE VERY DIFFERENT FROM THE OTHER MEN. SO, SHE BEGAN TO SPEND TIME GETTING TO KNOW THE SCHOOLTEACHER.

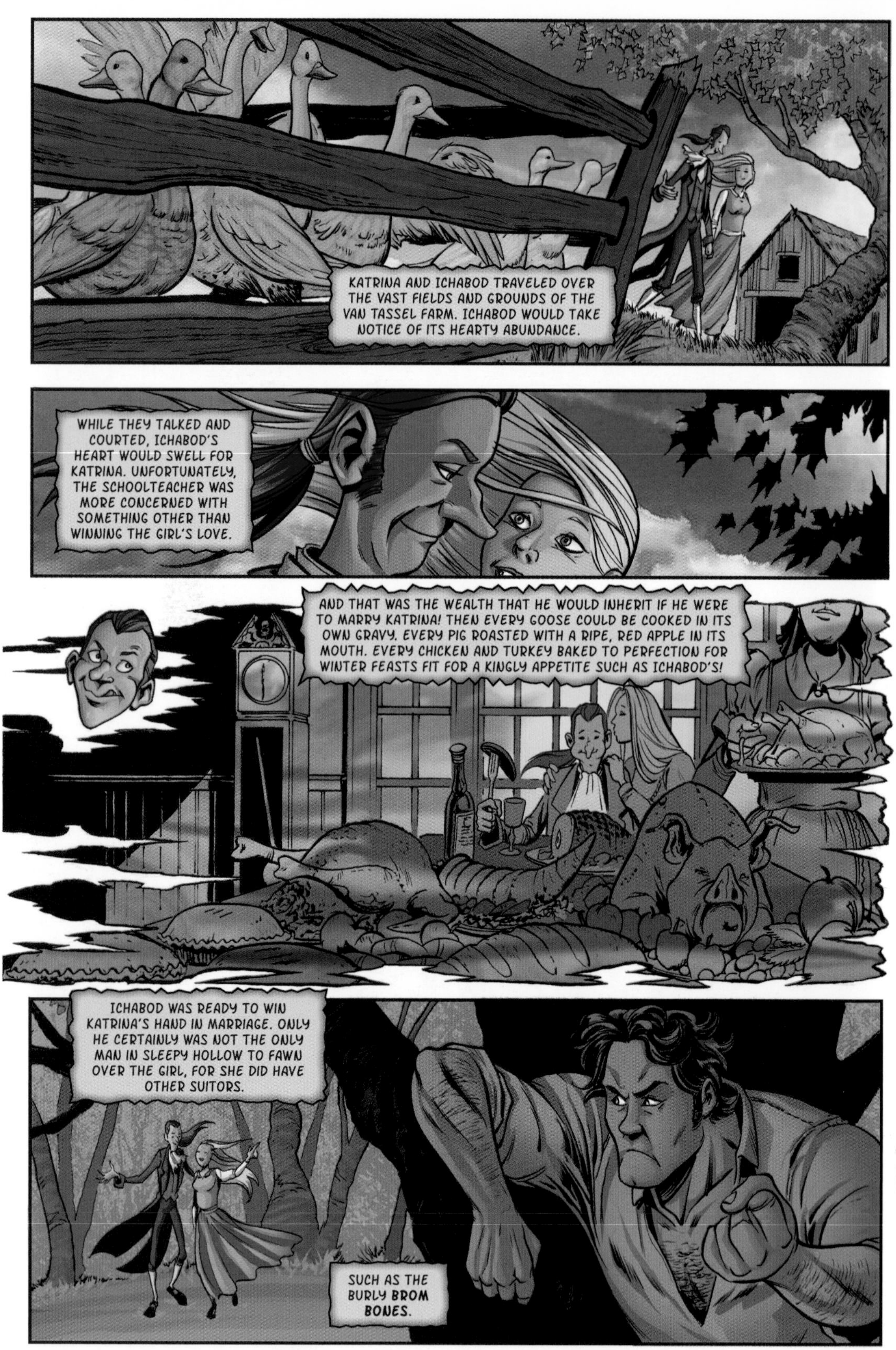
KATRINA AND ICHABOD TRAVELED OVER THE VAST FIELDS AND GROUNDS OF THE VAN TASSEL FARM. ICHABOD WOULD TAKE NOTICE OF ITS HEARTY ABUNDANCE.
WHILE THEY TALKED AND COURTED, ICHABOD'S HEART WOULD SWELL FOR KATRINA. UNFORTUNATELY, THE SCHOOLTEACHER WAS MORE CONCERNED WITH SOMETHING OTHER THAN WINNING THE GIRL'S LOVE.
AND THAT WAS THE WEALTH THAT HE WOULD INHERIT IF HE WERE TO MARRY KATRINA! THEN EVERY GOOSE COULD BE COOKED IN ITS OWN GRAVY. EVERY PIG ROASTED WITH A RIPE, RED APPLE IN ITS MOUTH. EVERY CHICKEN AND TURKEY BAKED TO PERFECTION FOR WINTER FEASTS FIT FOR A KINGLY APPETITE SUCH AS ICHABOD'S!
ICHABOD WAS READY TO WIN KATRINA'S HAND IN MARRIAGE. ONLY HE CERTAINLY WAS NOT THE ONLY MAN IN SLEEPY HOLLOW TO FAWN OVER THE GIRL, FOR SHE DID HAVE OTHER SUITORS.
SUCH AS THE BURLY **BROM BONES**.

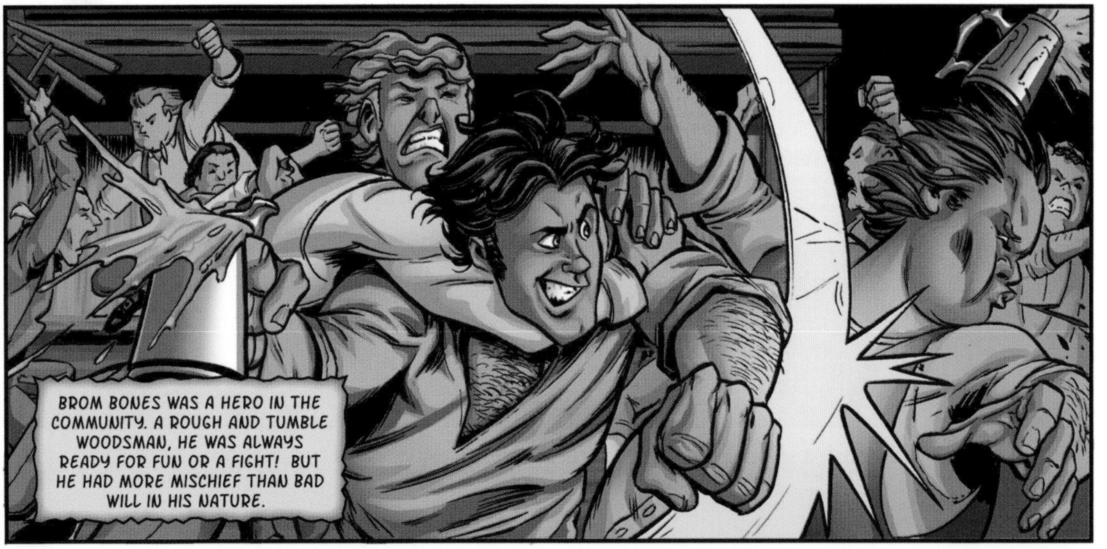
BROM BONES WAS A HERO IN THE COMMUNITY. A ROUGH AND TUMBLE WOODSMAN, HE WAS ALWAYS READY FOR FUN OR A FIGHT! BUT HE HAD MORE MISCHIEF THAN BAD WILL IN HIS NATURE.

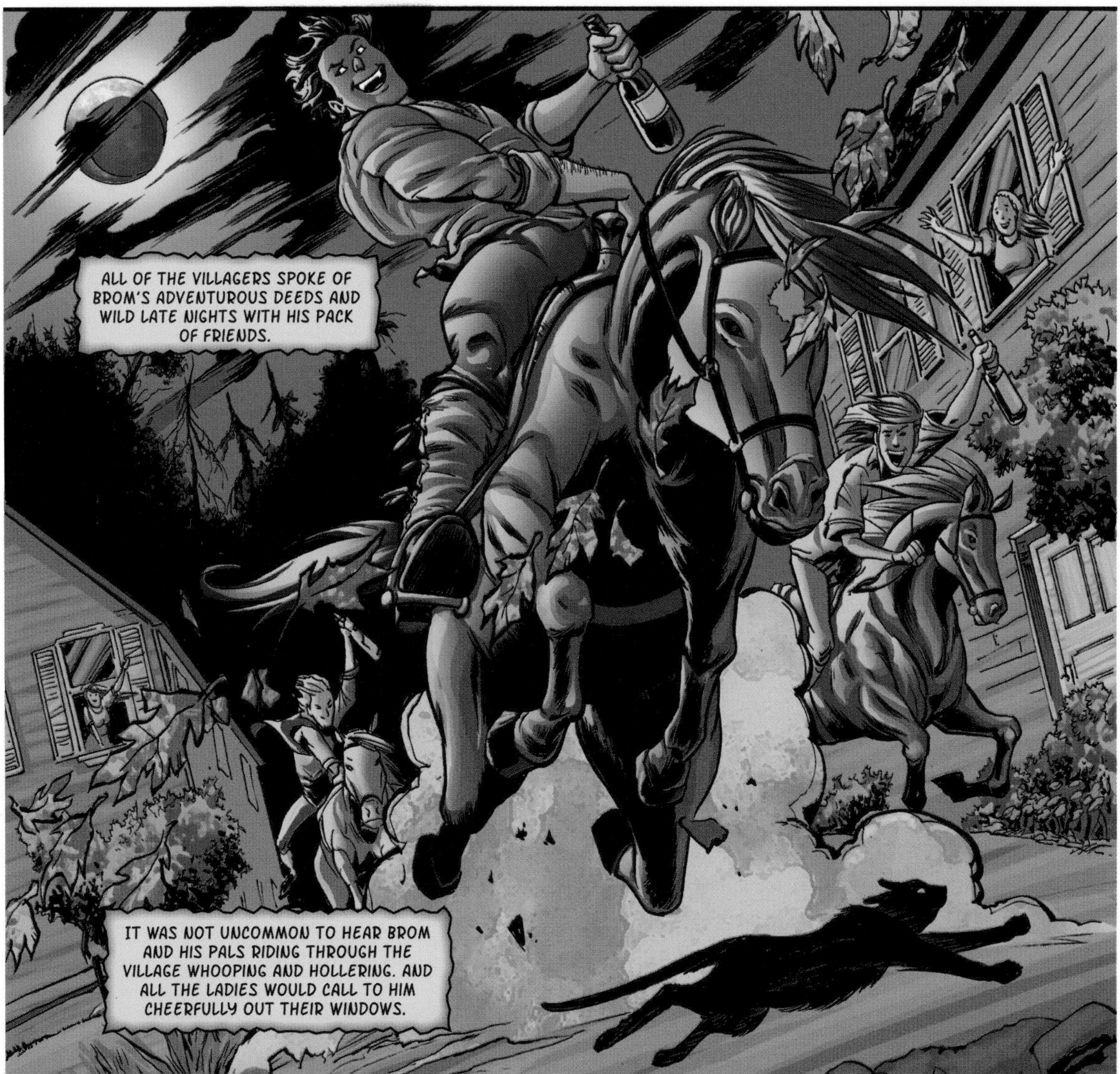
ALL OF THE VILLAGERS SPOKE OF BROM'S ADVENTUROUS DEEDS AND WILD LATE NIGHTS WITH HIS PACK OF FRIENDS.
IT WAS NOT UNCOMMON TO HEAR BROM AND HIS PALS RIDING THROUGH THE VILLAGE WHOOPING AND HOLLERING. AND ALL THE LADIES WOULD CALL TO HIM CHEERFULLY OUT THEIR WINDOWS.

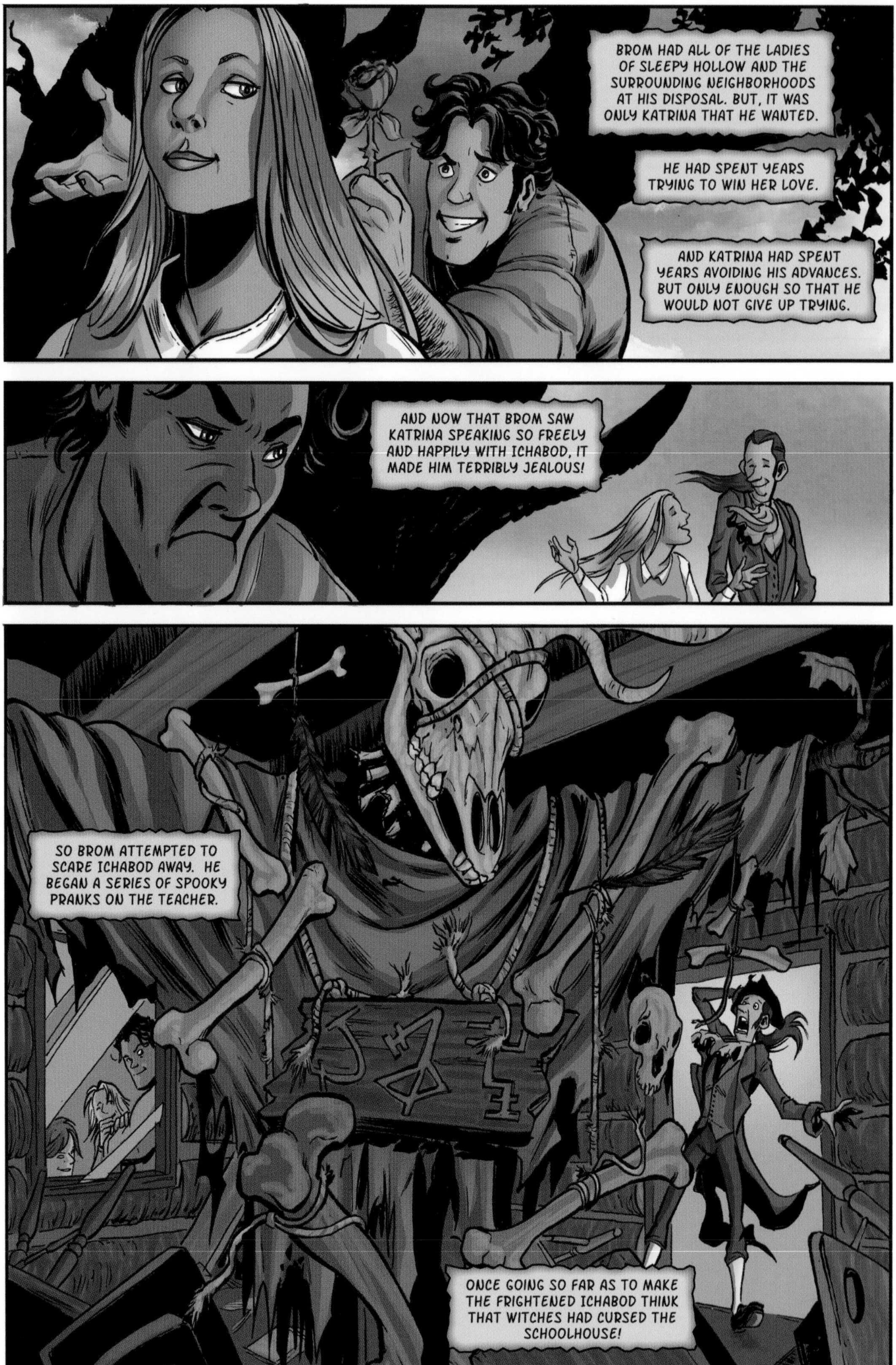
BROM HAD ALL OF THE LADIES OF SLEEPY HOLLOW AND THE SURROUNDING NEIGHBORHOODS AT HIS DISPOSAL. BUT, IT WAS ONLY KATRINA THAT HE WANTED.
HE HAD SPENT YEARS TRYING TO WIN HER LOVE.
AND KATRINA HAD SPENT YEARS AVOIDING HIS ADVANCES. BUT ONLY ENOUGH SO THAT HE WOULD NOT GIVE UP TRYING.
AND NOW THAT BROM SAW KATRINA SPEAKING SO FREELY AND HAPPILY WITH ICHABOD, IT MADE HIM TERRIBLY JEALOUS!
SO BROM ATTEMPTED TO SCARE ICHABOD AWAY. HE BEGAN A SERIES OF SPOOKY PRANKS ON THE TEACHER.
ONCE GOING SO FAR AS TO MAKE THE FRIGHTENED ICHABOD THINK THAT WITCHES HAD CURSED THE SCHOOLHOUSE!

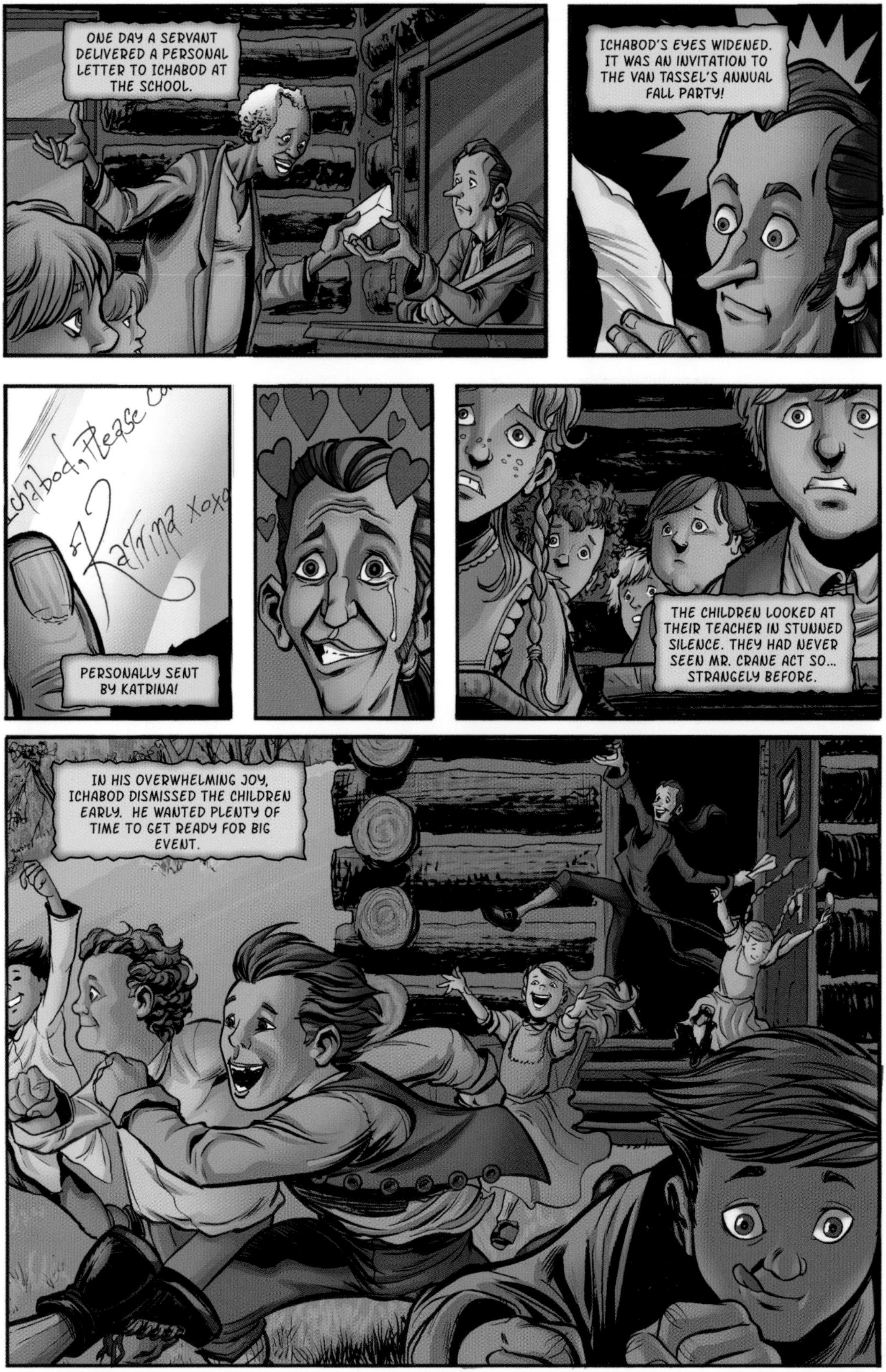
ONE DAY A SERVANT DELIVERED A PERSONAL LETTER TO ICHABOD AT THE SCHOOL.
ICHABOD'S EYES WIDENED. IT WAS AN INVITATION TO THE VAN TASSEL'S ANNUAL FALL PARTY!
Ichabod, Please Co
Katrina xoxo
PERSONALLY SENT BY KATRINA!
THE CHILDREN LOOKED AT THEIR TEACHER IN STUNNED SILENCE. THEY HAD NEVER SEEN MR. CRANE ACT SO... STRANGELY BEFORE.
IN HIS OVERWHELMING JOY, ICHABOD DISMISSED THE CHILDREN EARLY. HE WANTED PLENTY OF TIME TO GET READY FOR BIG EVENT.

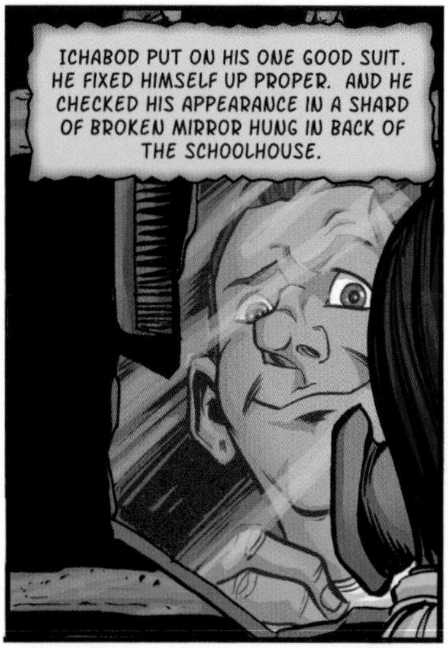
ICHABOD PUT ON HIS ONE GOOD SUIT. HE FIXED HIMSELF UP PROPER. AND HE CHECKED HIS APPEARANCE IN A SHARD OF BROKEN MIRROR HUNG IN BACK OF THE SCHOOLHOUSE.

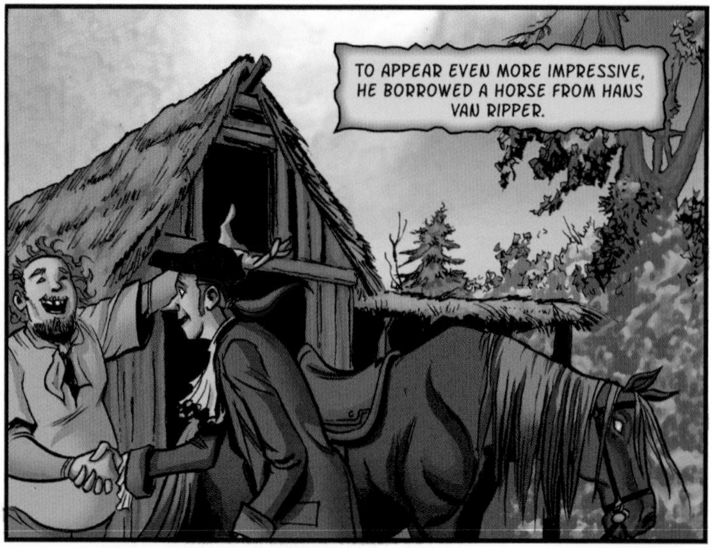
TO APPEAR EVEN MORE IMPRESSIVE, HE BORROWED A HORSE FROM HANS VAN RIPPER.

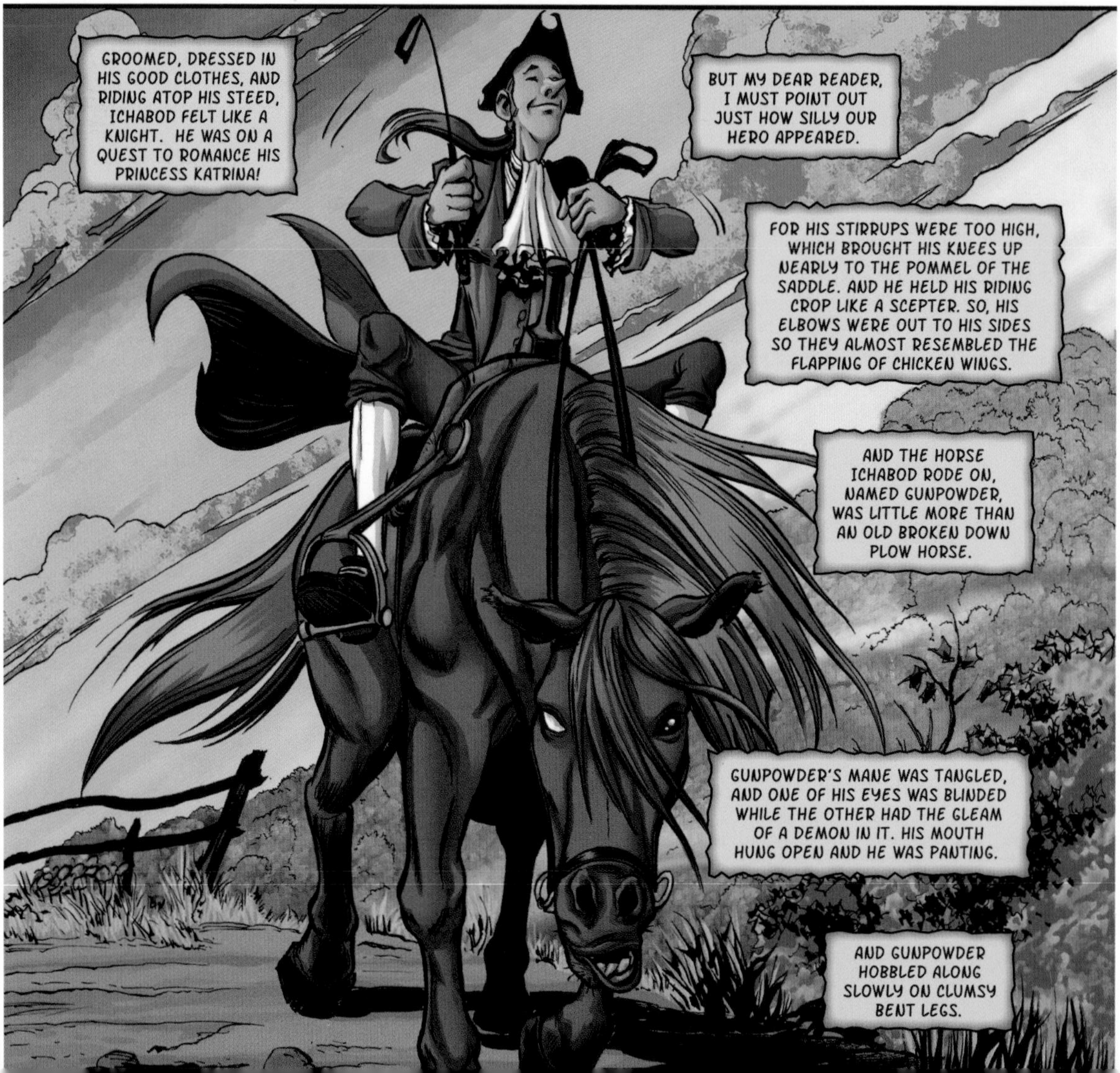
GROOMED, DRESSED IN HIS GOOD CLOTHES, AND RIDING ATOP HIS STEED, ICHABOD FELT LIKE A KNIGHT. HE WAS ON A QUEST TO ROMANCE HIS PRINCESS KATRINA!
BUT MY DEAR READER, I MUST POINT OUT JUST HOW SILLY OUR HERO APPEARED.
FOR HIS STIRRUPS WERE TOO HIGH, WHICH BROUGHT HIS KNEES UP NEARLY TO THE POMMEL OF THE SADDLE. AND HE HELD HIS RIDING CROP LIKE A SCEPTER. SO, HIS ELBOWS WERE OUT TO HIS SIDES SO THEY ALMOST RESEMBLED THE FLAPPING OF CHICKEN WINGS.
AND THE HORSE ICHABOD RODE ON, NAMED GUNPOWDER, WAS LITTLE MORE THAN AN OLD BROKEN DOWN PLOW HORSE.
GUNPOWDER'S MANE WAS TANGLED, AND ONE OF HIS EYES WAS BLINDED WHILE THE OTHER HAD THE GLEAM OF A DEMON IN IT. HIS MOUTH HUNG OPEN AND HE WAS PANTING.
AND GUNPOWDER HOBBLED ALONG SLOWLY ON CLUMSY BENT LEGS.

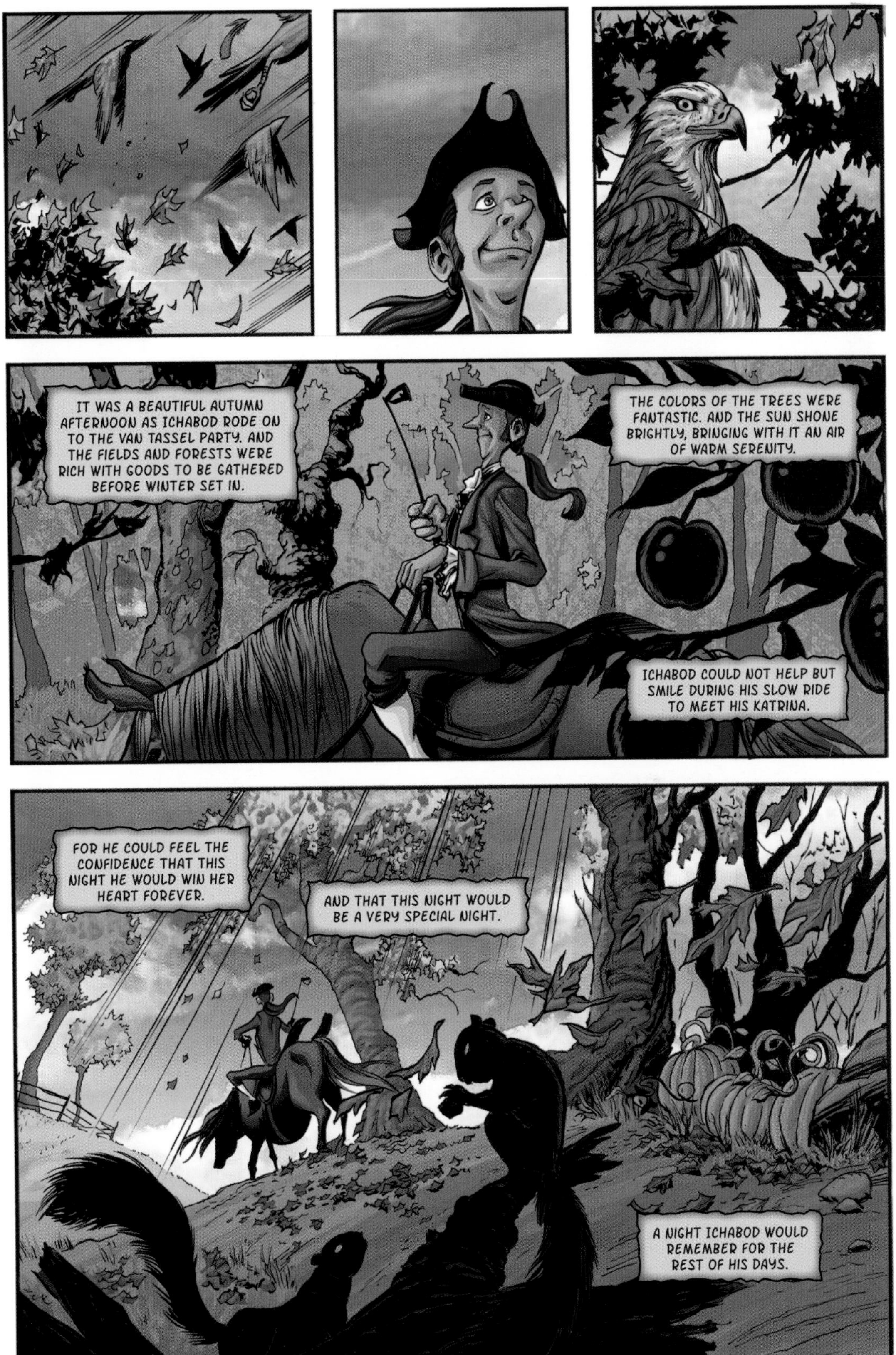
IT WAS A BEAUTIFUL AUTUMN AFTERNOON AS ICHABOD RODE ON TO THE VAN TASSEL PARTY. AND THE FIELDS AND FORESTS WERE RICH WITH GOODS TO BE GATHERED BEFORE WINTER SET IN.
THE COLORS OF THE TREES WERE FANTASTIC. AND THE SUN SHONE BRIGHTLY, BRINGING WITH IT AN AIR OF WARM SERENITY.
ICHABOD COULD NOT HELP BUT SMILE DURING HIS SLOW RIDE TO MEET HIS KATRINA.
FOR HE COULD FEEL THE CONFIDENCE THAT THIS NIGHT HE WOULD WIN HER HEART FOREVER.
AND THAT THIS NIGHT WOULD BE A VERY SPECIAL NIGHT.
A NIGHT ICHABOD WOULD REMEMBER FOR THE REST OF HIS DAYS.

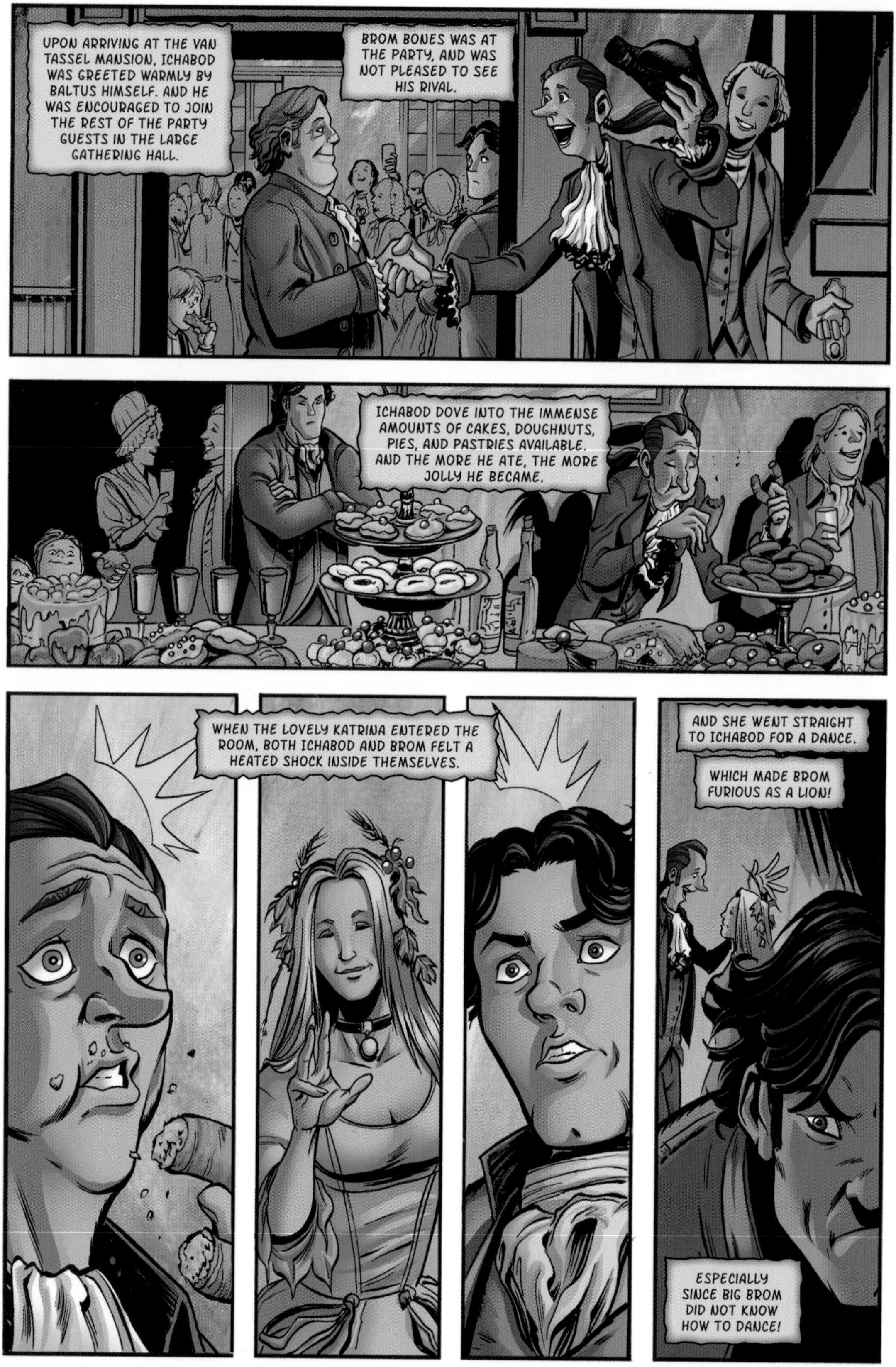
UPON ARRIVING AT THE VAN TASSEL MANSION, ICHABOD WAS GREETED WARMLY BY BALTUS HIMSELF. AND HE WAS ENCOURAGED TO JOIN THE REST OF THE PARTY GUESTS IN THE LARGE GATHERING HALL.
BROM BONES WAS AT THE PARTY, AND WAS NOT PLEASED TO SEE HIS RIVAL.
ICHABOD DOVE INTO THE IMMENSE AMOUNTS OF CAKES, DOUGHNUTS, PIES, AND PASTRIES AVAILABLE. AND THE MORE HE ATE, THE MORE JOLLY HE BECAME.
WHEN THE LOVELY KATRINA ENTERED THE ROOM, BOTH ICHABOD AND BROM FELT A HEATED SHOCK INSIDE THEMSELVES.
AND SHE WENT STRAIGHT TO ICHABOD FOR A DANCE.
WHICH MADE BROM FURIOUS AS A LION!
ESPECIALLY SINCE BIG BROM DID NOT KNOW HOW TO DANCE!

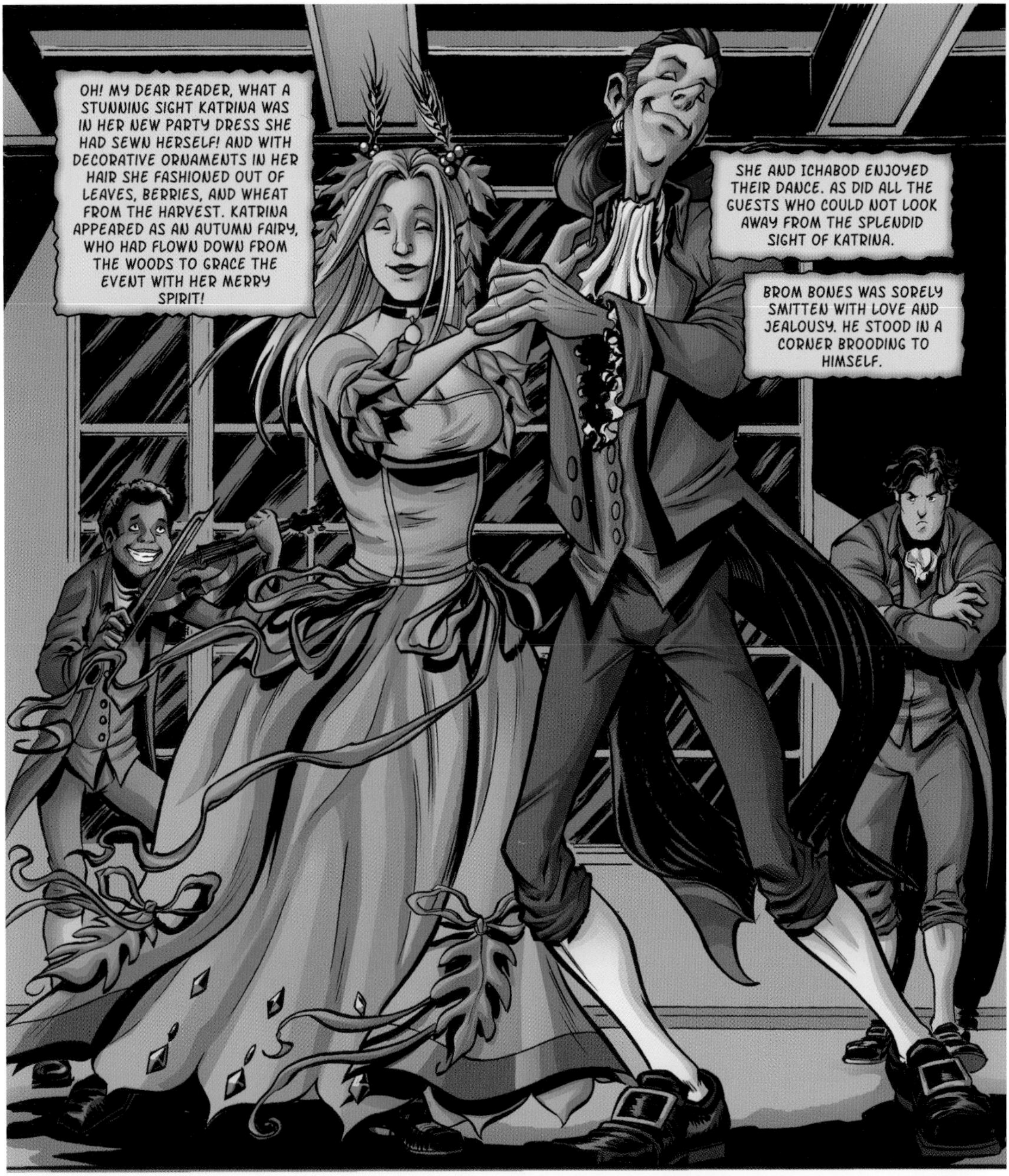
OH! MY DEAR READER, WHAT A STUNNING SIGHT KATRINA WAS IN HER NEW PARTY DRESS SHE HAD SEWN HERSELF! AND WITH DECORATIVE ORNAMENTS IN HER HAIR SHE FASHIONED OUT OF LEAVES, BERRIES, AND WHEAT FROM THE HARVEST. KATRINA APPEARED AS AN AUTUMN FAIRY, WHO HAD FLOWN DOWN FROM THE WOODS TO GRACE THE EVENT WITH HER MERRY SPIRIT!
SHE AND ICHABOD ENJOYED THEIR DANCE. AS DID ALL THE GUESTS WHO COULD NOT LOOK AWAY FROM THE SPLENDID SIGHT OF KATRINA.
BROM BONES WAS SORELY SMITTEN WITH LOVE AND JEALOUSY. HE STOOD IN A CORNER BROODING TO HIMSELF.

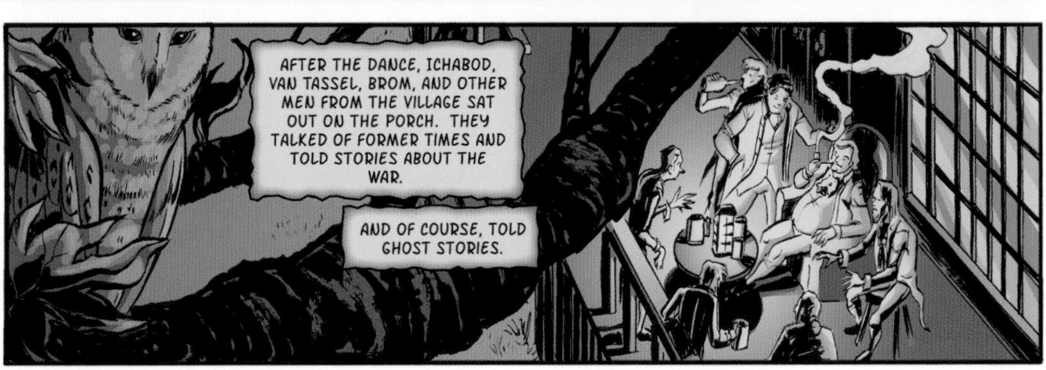
AFTER THE DANCE, ICHABOD, VAN TASSEL, BROM, AND OTHER MEN FROM THE VILLAGE SAT OUT ON THE PORCH. THEY TALKED OF FORMER TIMES AND TOLD STORIES ABOUT THE WAR.
AND OF COURSE, TOLD GHOST STORIES.

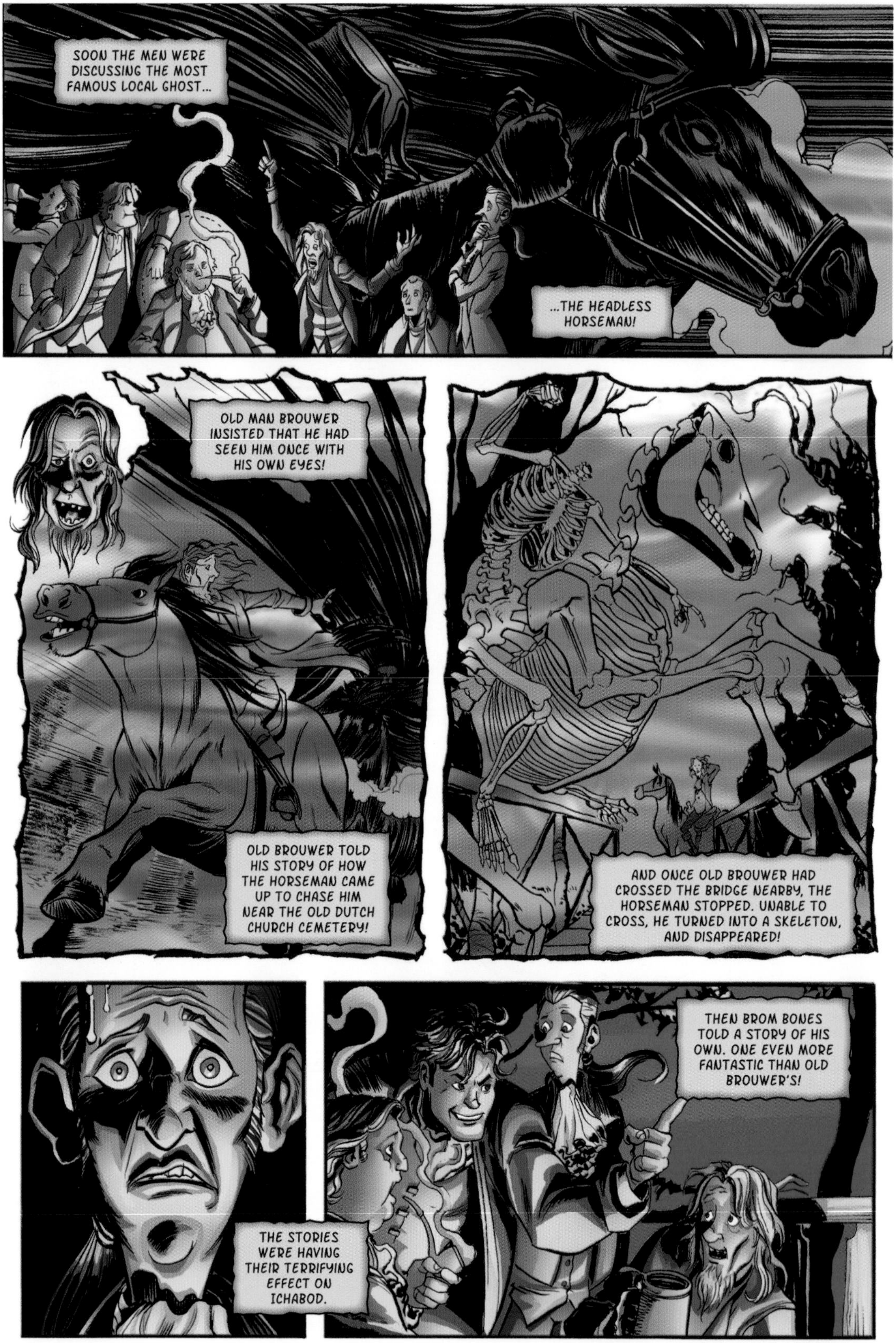
SOON THE MEN WERE DISCUSSING THE MOST FAMOUS LOCAL GHOST...
...THE HEADLESS HORSEMAN!
OLD MAN BROUWER INSISTED THAT HE HAD SEEN HIM ONCE WITH HIS OWN EYES!
OLD BROUWER TOLD HIS STORY OF HOW THE HORSEMAN CAME UP TO CHASE HIM NEAR THE OLD DUTCH CHURCH CEMETERY!
AND ONCE OLD BROUWER HAD CROSSED THE BRIDGE NEARBY, THE HORSEMAN STOPPED. UNABLE TO CROSS, HE TURNED INTO A SKELETON, AND DISAPPEARED!
THE STORIES WERE HAVING THEIR TERRIFYING EFFECT ON ICHABOD.
THEN BROM BONES TOLD A STORY OF HIS OWN. ONE EVEN MORE FANTASTIC THAN OLD BROUWER'S!

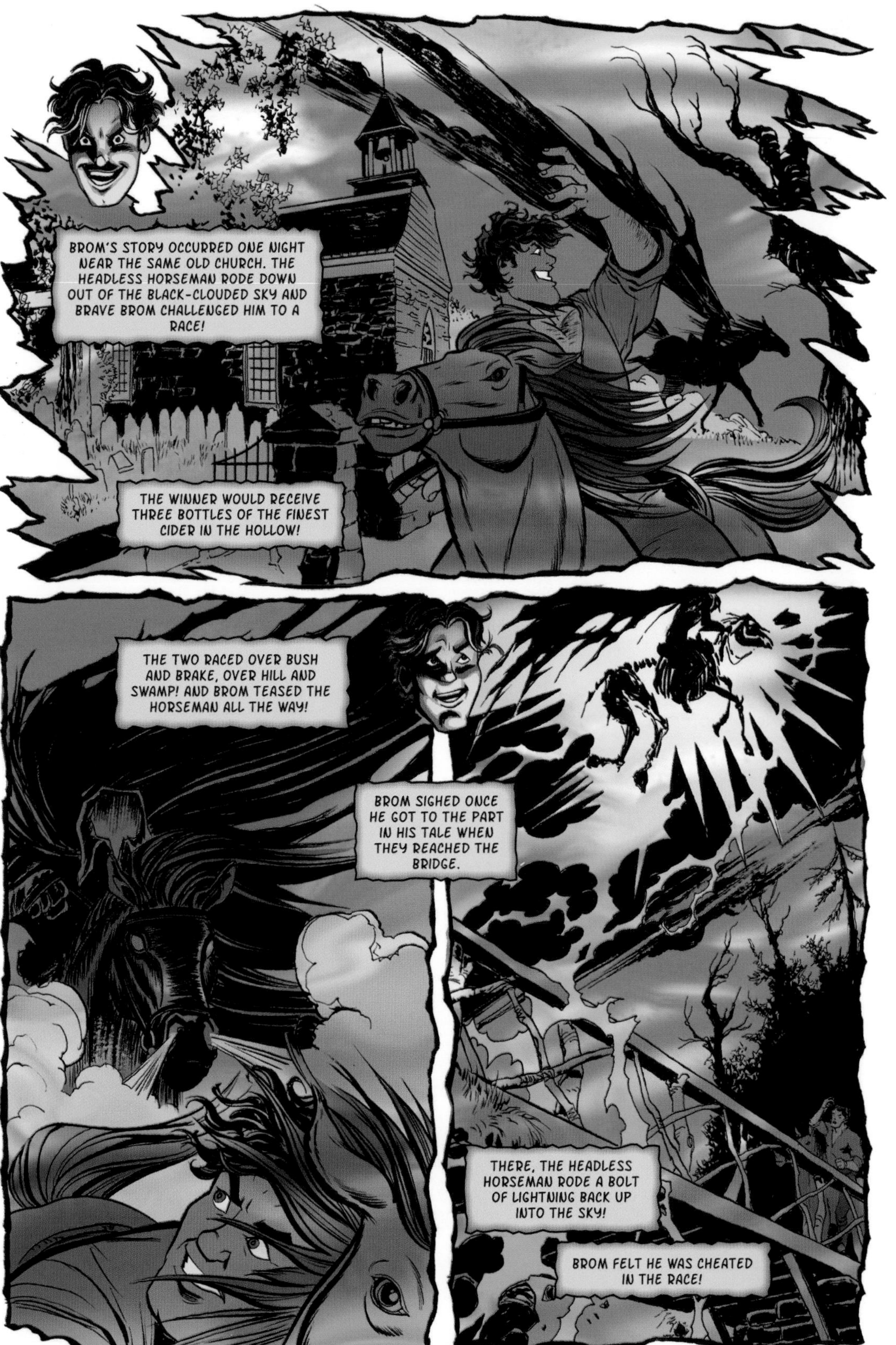
BROM'S STORY OCCURRED ONE NIGHT NEAR THE SAME OLD CHURCH. THE HEADLESS HORSEMAN RODE DOWN OUT OF THE BLACK-CLOUDED SKY AND BRAVE BROM CHALLENGED HIM TO A RACE!
THE WINNER WOULD RECEIVE THREE BOTTLES OF THE FINEST CIDER IN THE HOLLOW!
THE TWO RACED OVER BUSH AND BRAKE, OVER HILL AND SWAMP! AND BROM TEASED THE HORSEMAN ALL THE WAY!
BROM SIGHED ONCE HE GOT TO THE PART IN HIS TALE WHEN THEY REACHED THE BRIDGE.
THERE, THE HEADLESS HORSEMAN RODE A BOLT OF LIGHTNING BACK UP INTO THE SKY!
BROM FELT HE WAS CHEATED IN THE RACE!

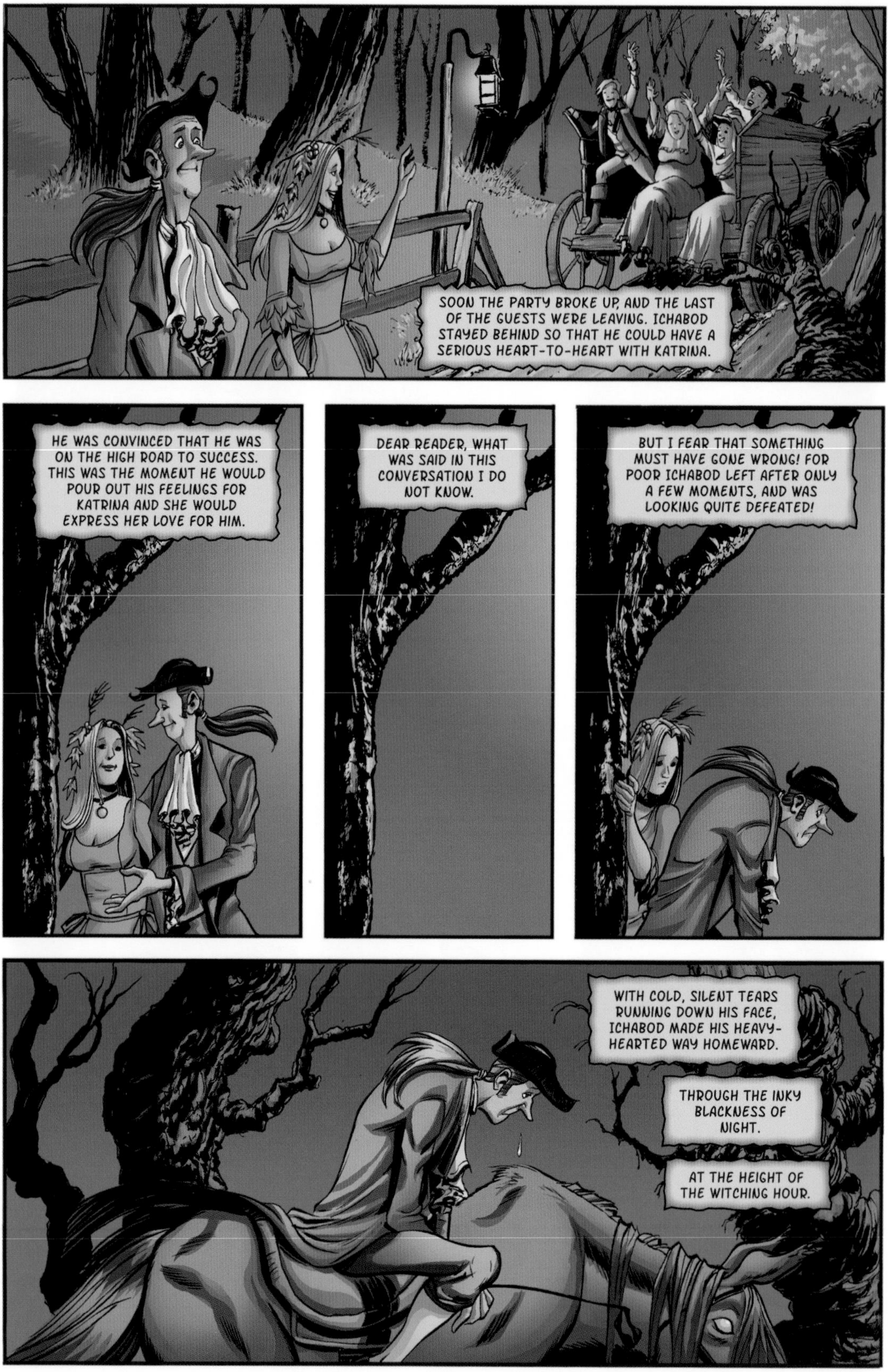
SOON THE PARTY BROKE UP, AND THE LAST OF THE GUESTS WERE LEAVING. ICHABOD STAYED BEHIND SO THAT HE COULD HAVE A SERIOUS HEART-TO-HEART WITH KATRINA.
HE WAS CONVINCED THAT HE WAS ON THE HIGH ROAD TO SUCCESS. THIS WAS THE MOMENT HE WOULD POUR OUT HIS FEELINGS FOR KATRINA AND SHE WOULD EXPRESS HER LOVE FOR HIM.
DEAR READER, WHAT WAS SAID IN THIS CONVERSATION I DO NOT KNOW.
BUT I FEAR THAT SOMETHING MUST HAVE GONE WRONG! FOR POOR ICHABOD LEFT AFTER ONLY A FEW MOMENTS, AND WAS LOOKING QUITE DEFEATED!
WITH COLD, SILENT TEARS RUNNING DOWN HIS FACE, ICHABOD MADE HIS HEAVY-HEARTED WAY HOMEWARD.
THROUGH THE INKY BLACKNESS OF NIGHT.
AT THE HEIGHT OF THE WITCHING HOUR.

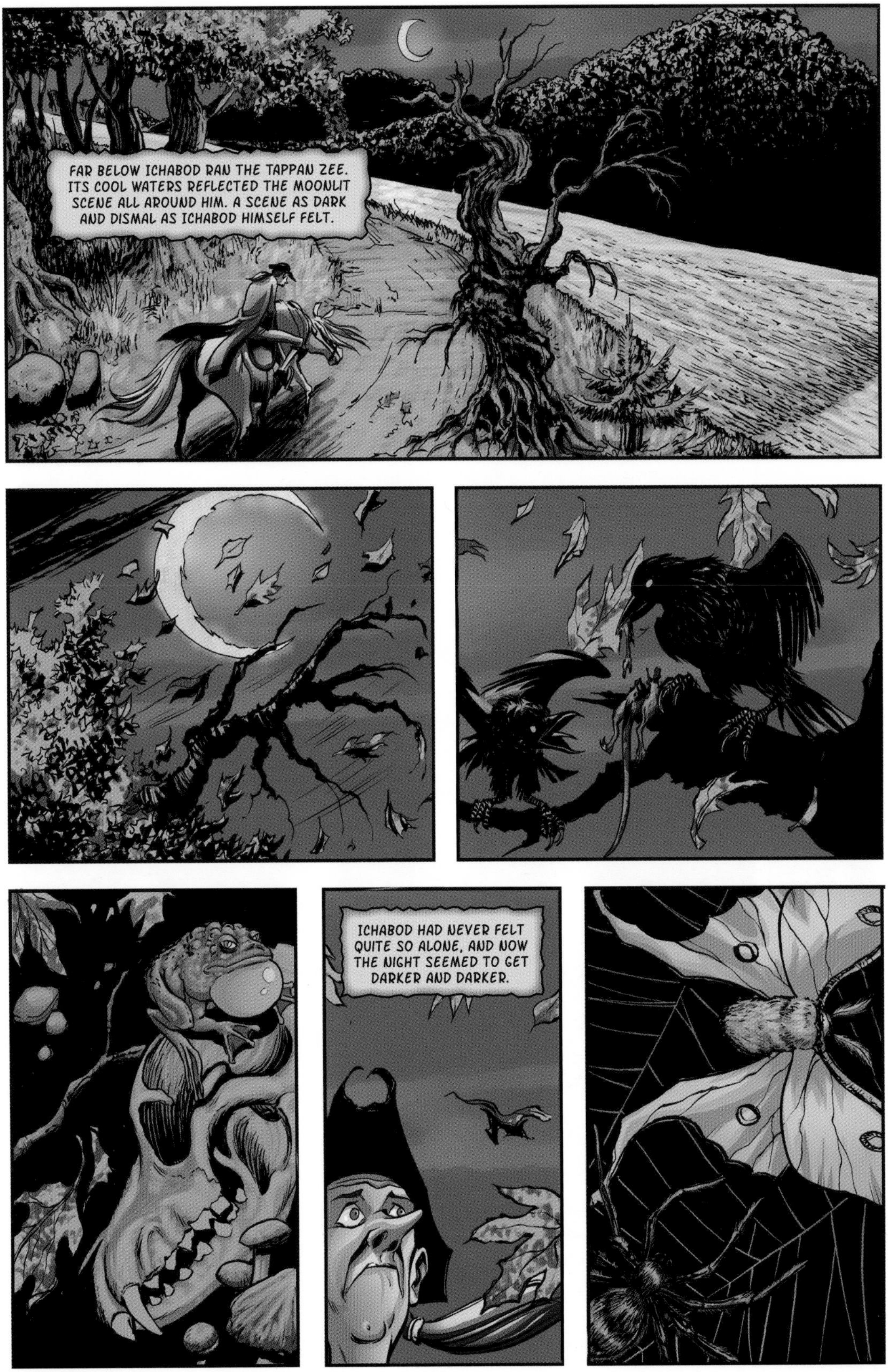
FAR BELOW ICHABOD RAN THE TAPPAN ZEE. ITS COOL WATERS REFLECTED THE MOONLIT SCENE ALL AROUND HIM. A SCENE AS DARK AND DISMAL AS ICHABOD HIMSELF FELT.
ICHABOD HAD NEVER FELT QUITE SO ALONE, AND NOW THE NIGHT SEEMED TO GET DARKER AND DARKER.

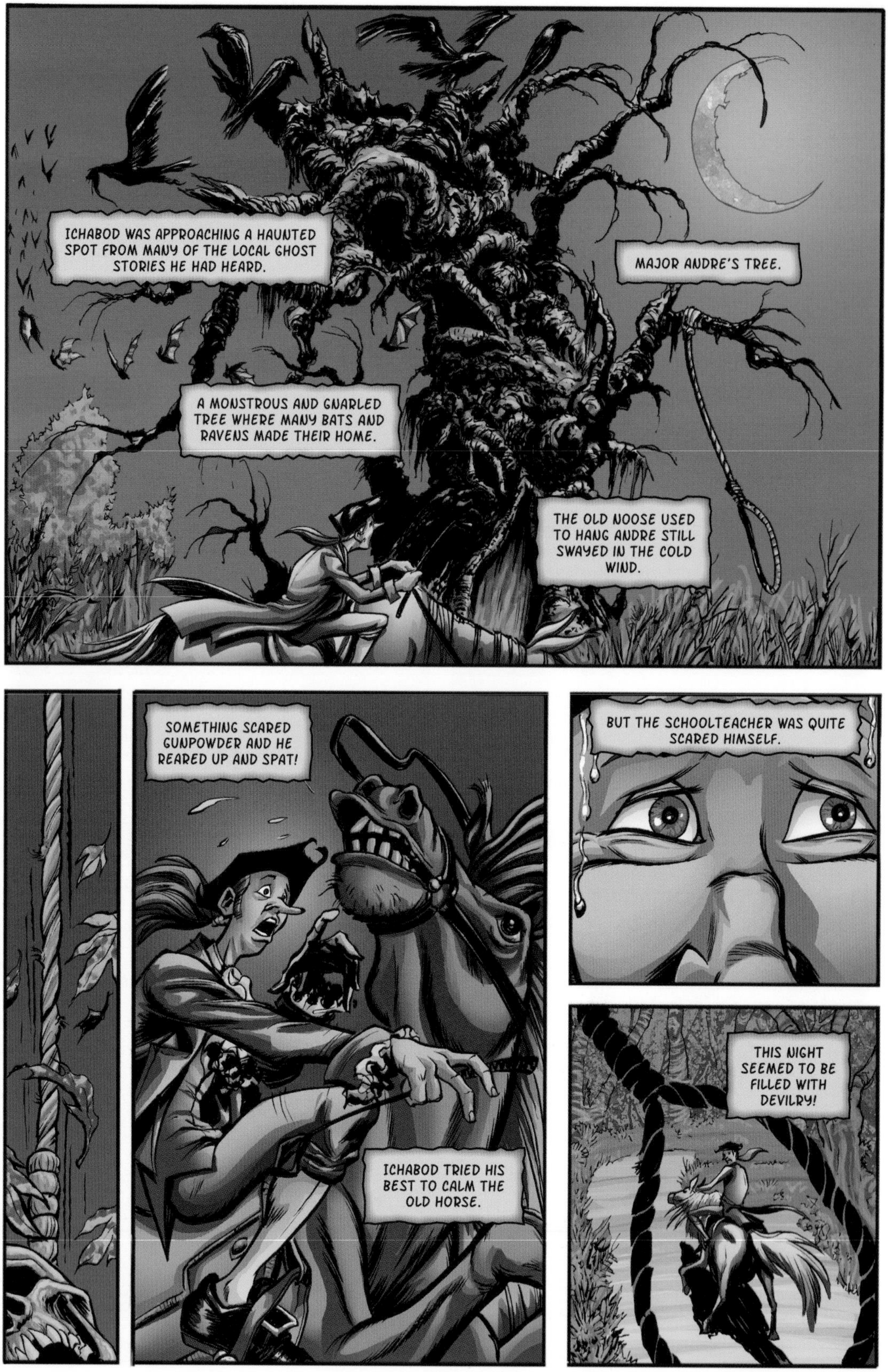
ICHABOD WAS APPROACHING A HAUNTED SPOT FROM MANY OF THE LOCAL GHOST STORIES HE HAD HEARD.
MAJOR ANDRE'S TREE.
A MONSTROUS AND GNARLED TREE WHERE MANY BATS AND RAVENS MADE THEIR HOME.
THE OLD NOOSE USED TO HANG ANDRE STILL SWAYED IN THE COLD WIND.
SOMETHING SCARED GUNPOWDER AND HE REARED UP AND SPAT!
ICHABOD TRIED HIS BEST TO CALM THE OLD HORSE.
BUT THE SCHOOLTEACHER WAS QUITE SCARED HIMSELF.
THIS NIGHT SEEMED TO BE FILLED WITH DEVILRY!

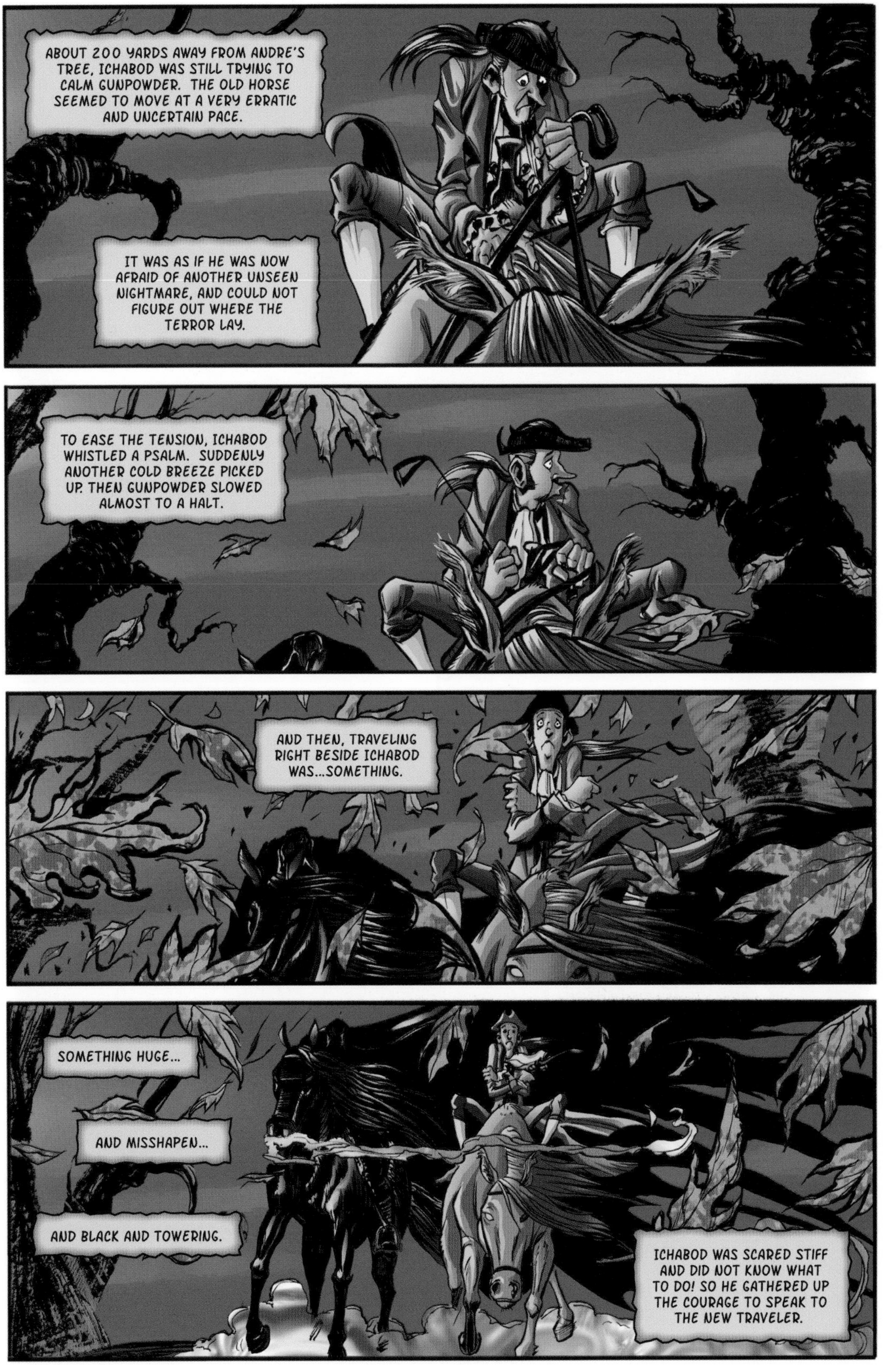
ABOUT 200 YARDS AWAY FROM ANDRE'S TREE, ICHABOD WAS STILL TRYING TO CALM GUNPOWDER. THE OLD HORSE SEEMED TO MOVE AT A VERY ERRATIC AND UNCERTAIN PACE.
IT WAS AS IF HE WAS NOW AFRAID OF ANOTHER UNSEEN NIGHTMARE, AND COULD NOT FIGURE OUT WHERE THE TERROR LAY.
TO EASE THE TENSION, ICHABOD WHISTLED A PSALM. SUDDENLY ANOTHER COLD BREEZE PICKED UP. THEN GUNPOWDER SLOWED ALMOST TO A HALT.
AND THEN, TRAVELING RIGHT BESIDE ICHABOD WAS...SOMETHING.
SOMETHING HUGE...
AND MISSHAPEN...
AND BLACK AND TOWERING.
ICHABOD WAS SCARED STIFF AND DID NOT KNOW WHAT TO DO! SO HE GATHERED UP THE COURAGE TO SPEAK TO THE NEW TRAVELER.

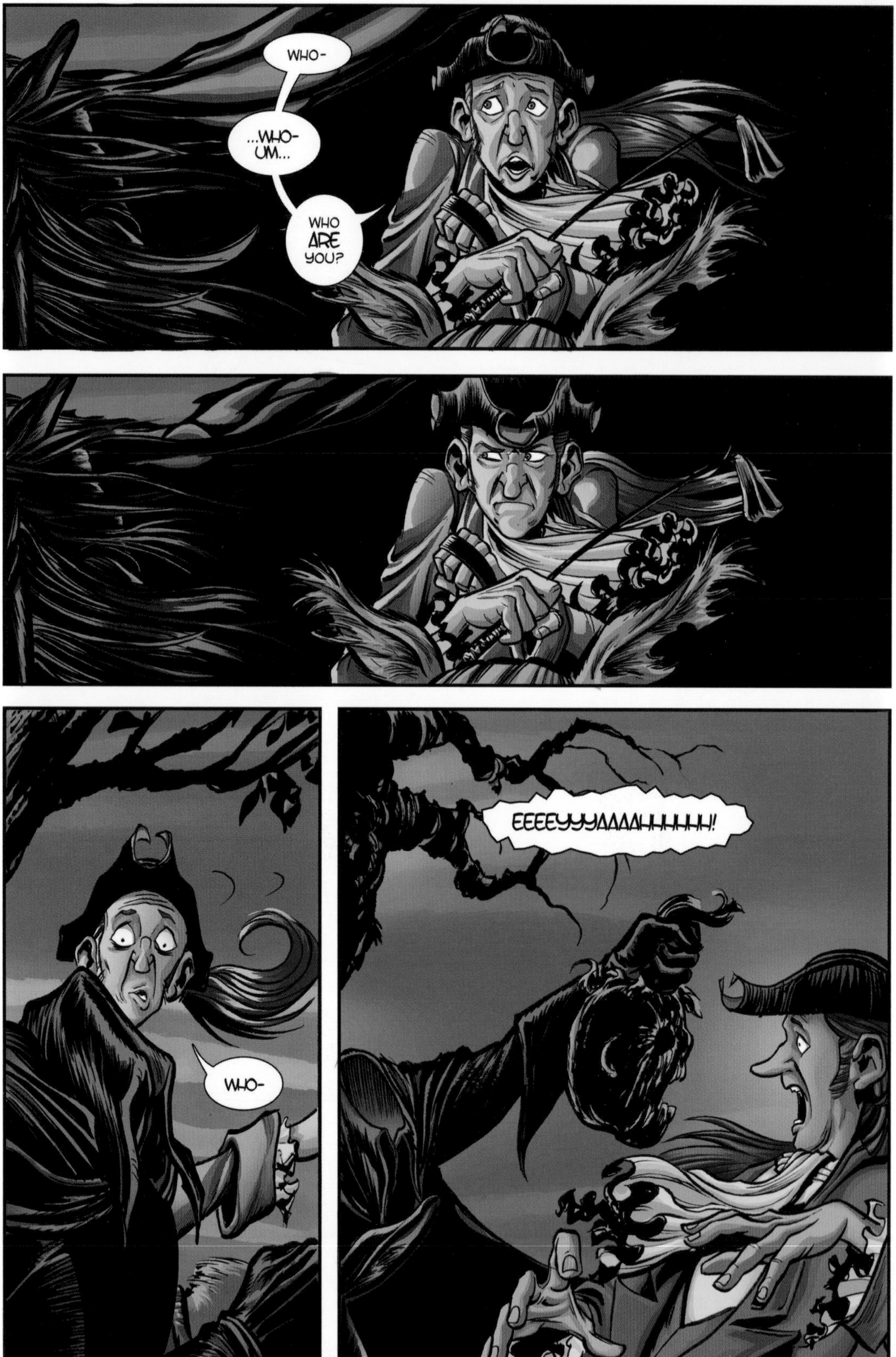
WHO-
...WHO-UM...
WHO ARE YOU?
WHO-
EEEEYYYAAAAHHHHHH!

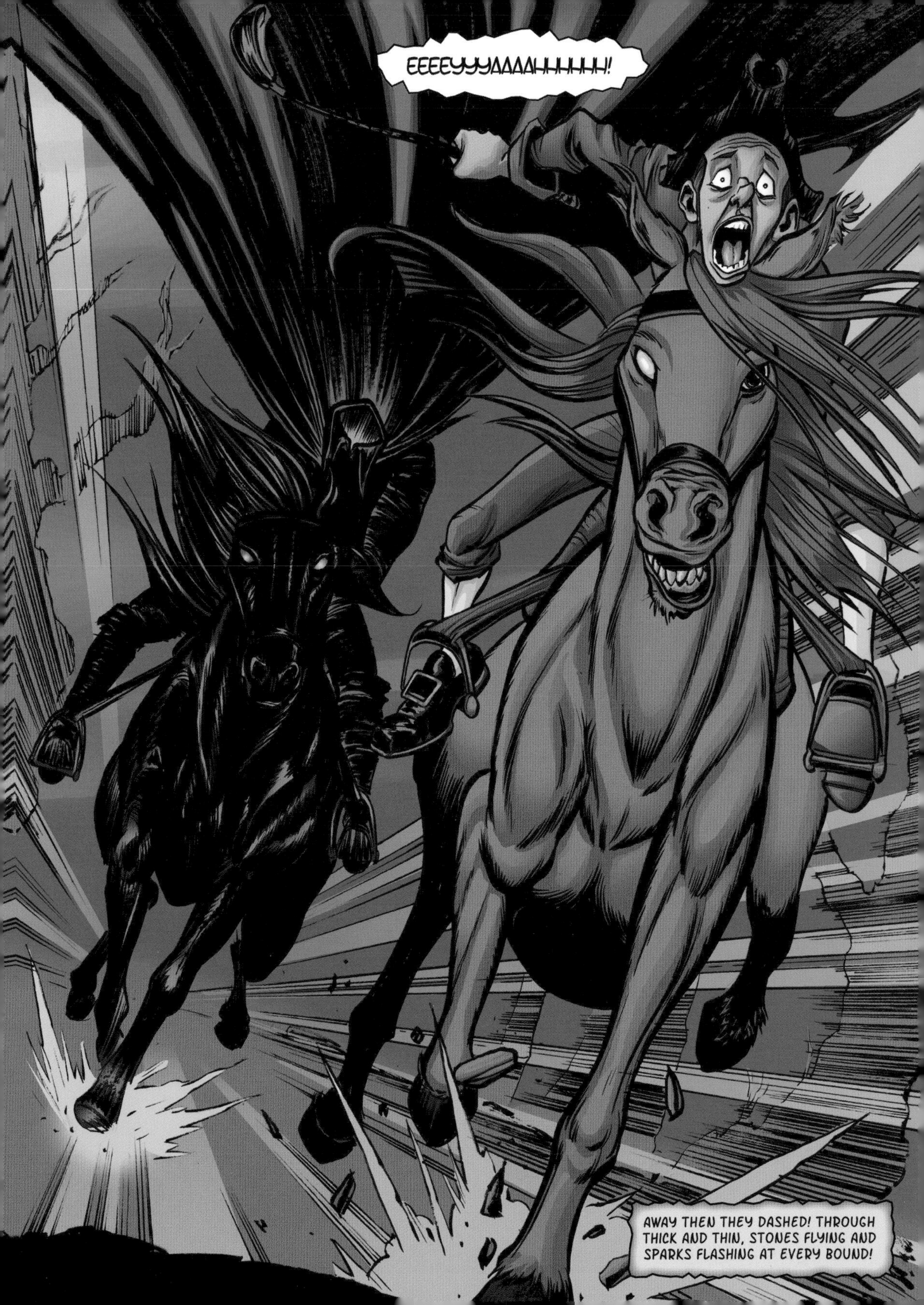
EEEEYYYAAAAHHHHHH!
AWAY THEN THEY DASHED! THROUGH THICK AND THIN, STONES FLYING AND SPARKS FLASHING AT EVERY BOUND!

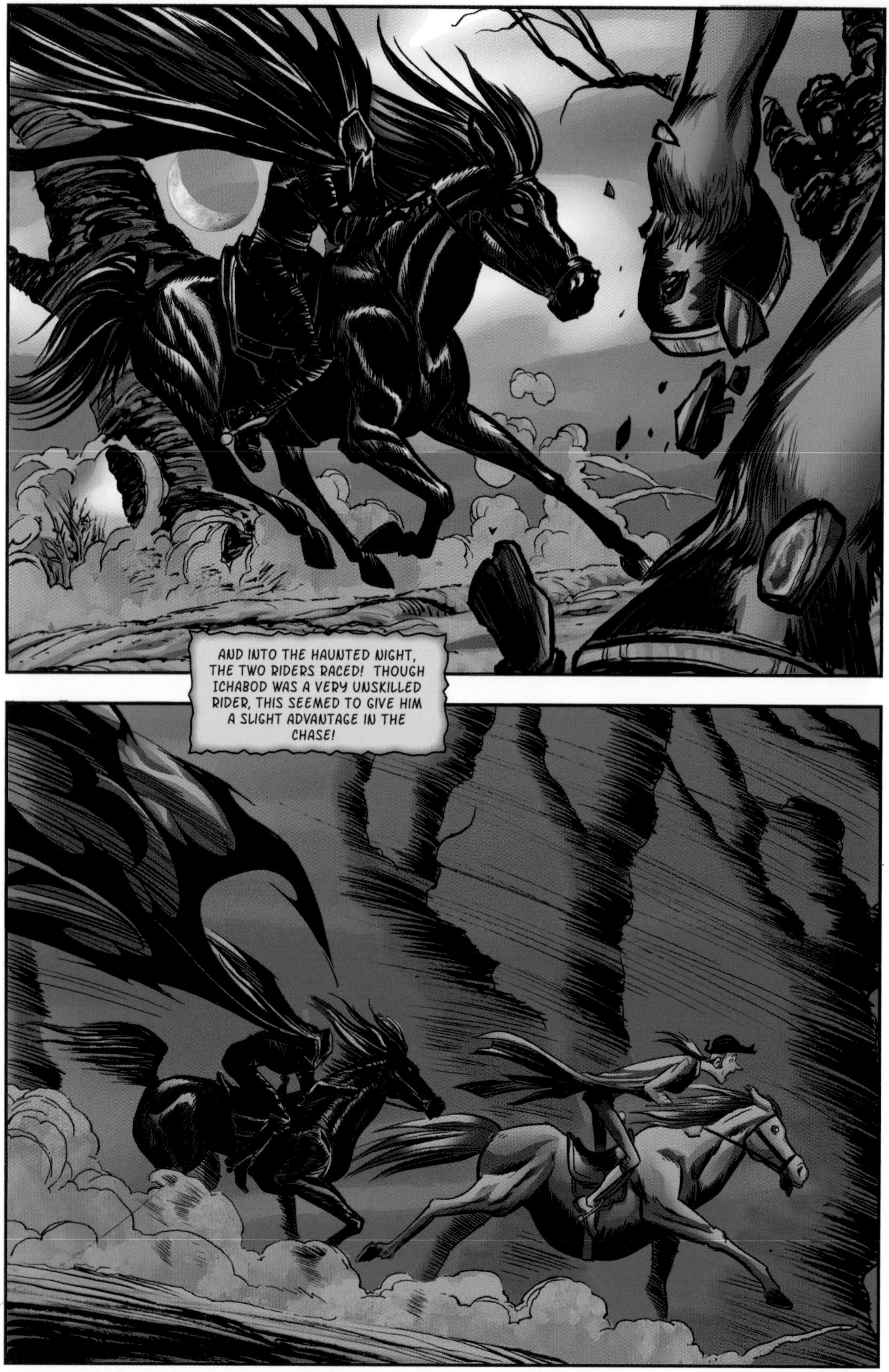
AND INTO THE HAUNTED NIGHT, THE TWO RIDERS RACED! THOUGH ICHABOD WAS A VERY UNSKILLED RIDER, THIS SEEMED TO GIVE HIM A SLIGHT ADVANTAGE IN THE CHASE!

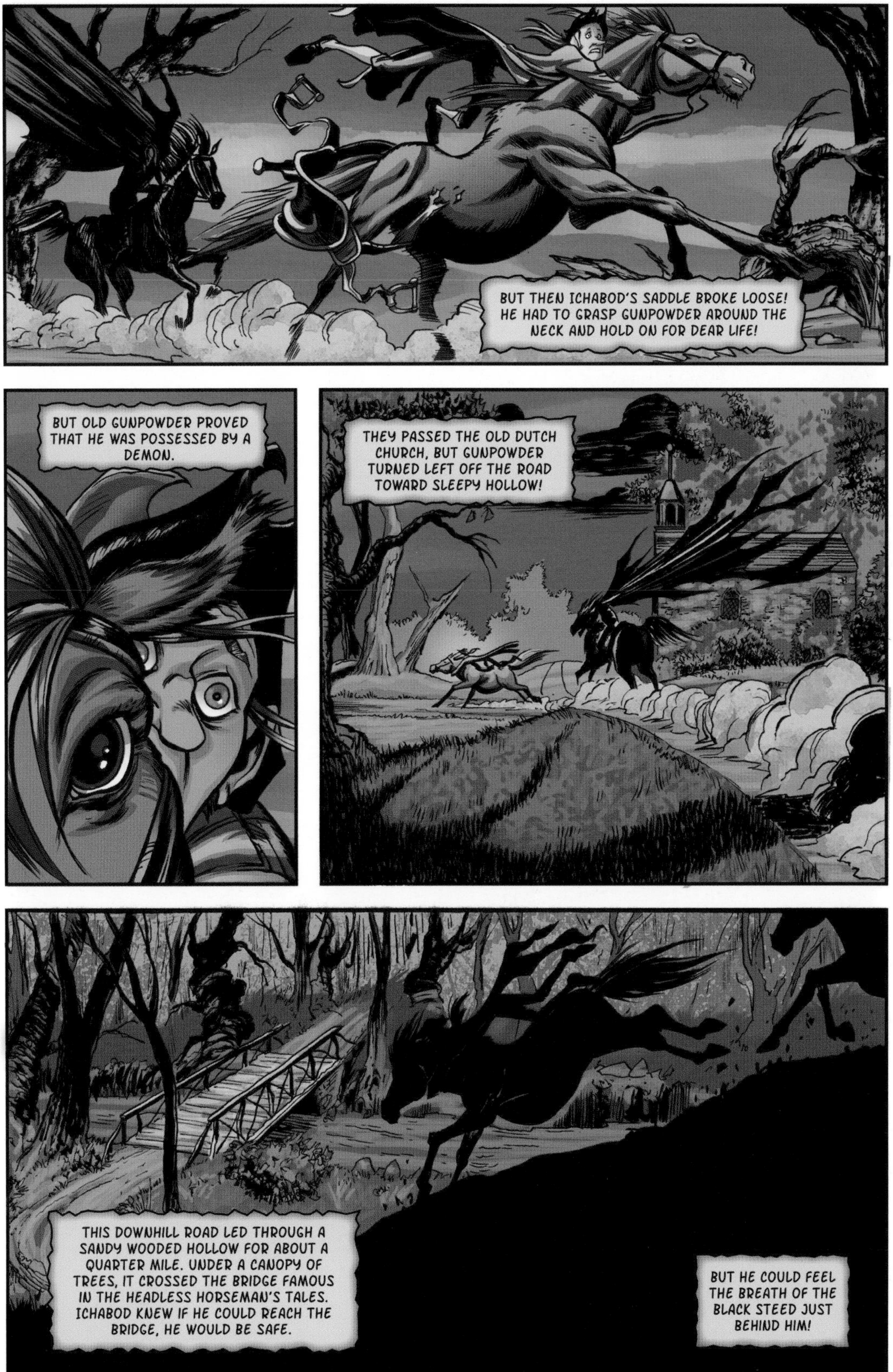
BUT THEN ICHABOD'S SADDLE BROKE LOOSE! HE HAD TO GRASP GUNPOWDER AROUND THE NECK AND HOLD ON FOR DEAR LIFE!
BUT OLD GUNPOWDER PROVED THAT HE WAS POSSESSED BY A DEMON.
THEY PASSED THE OLD DUTCH CHURCH, BUT GUNPOWDER TURNED LEFT OFF THE ROAD TOWARD SLEEPY HOLLOW!
THIS DOWNHILL ROAD LED THROUGH A SANDY WOODED HOLLOW FOR ABOUT A QUARTER MILE. UNDER A CANOPY OF TREES, IT CROSSED THE BRIDGE FAMOUS IN THE HEADLESS HORSEMAN'S TALES. ICHABOD KNEW IF HE COULD REACH THE BRIDGE, HE WOULD BE SAFE.
BUT HE COULD FEEL THE BREATH OF THE BLACK STEED JUST BEHIND HIM!

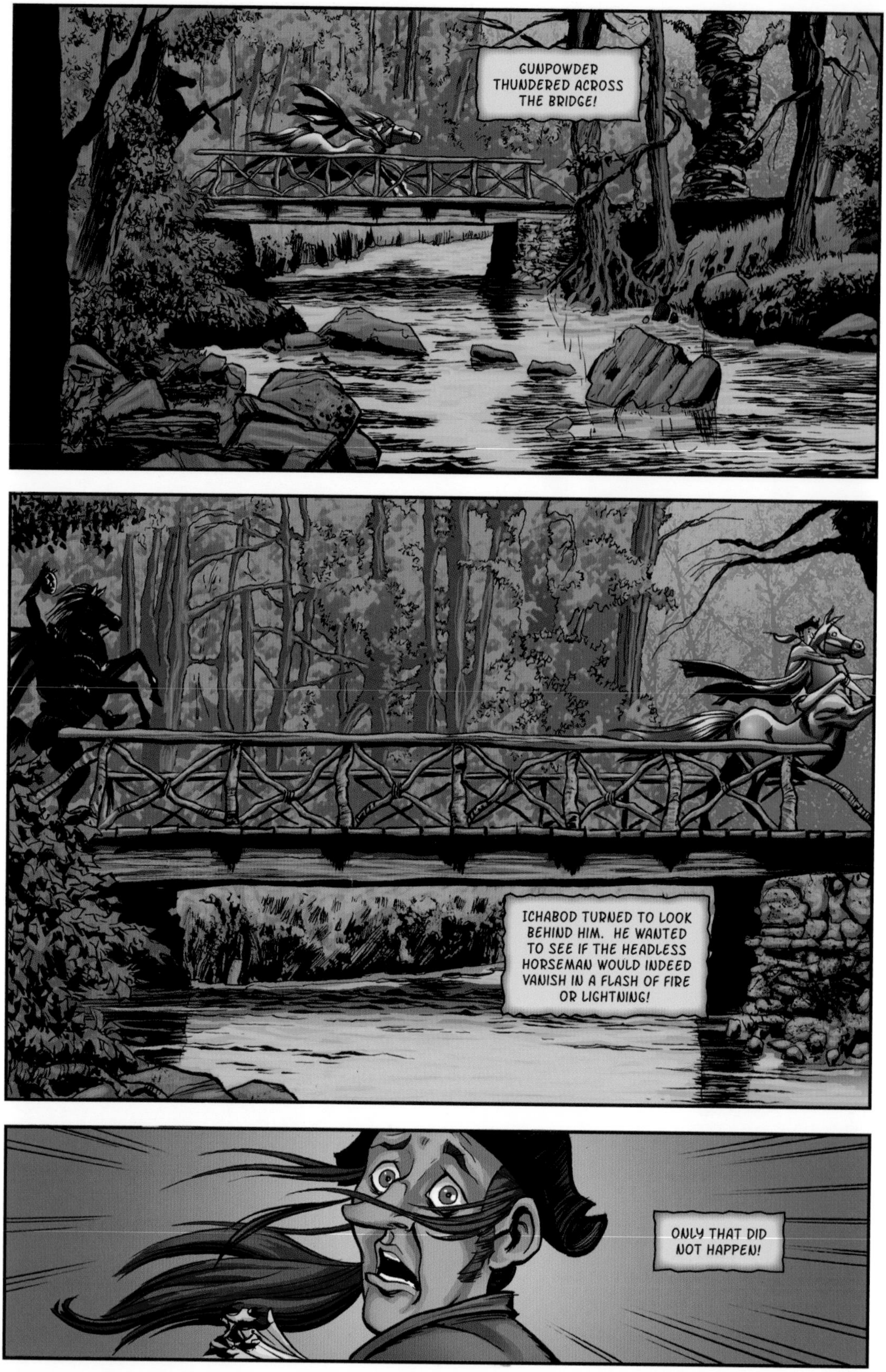
GUNPOWDER THUNDERED ACROSS THE BRIDGE!
ICHABOD TURNED TO LOOK BEHIND HIM. HE WANTED TO SEE IF THE HEADLESS HORSEMAN WOULD INDEED VANISH IN A FLASH OF FIRE OR LIGHTNING!
ONLY THAT DID NOT HAPPEN!

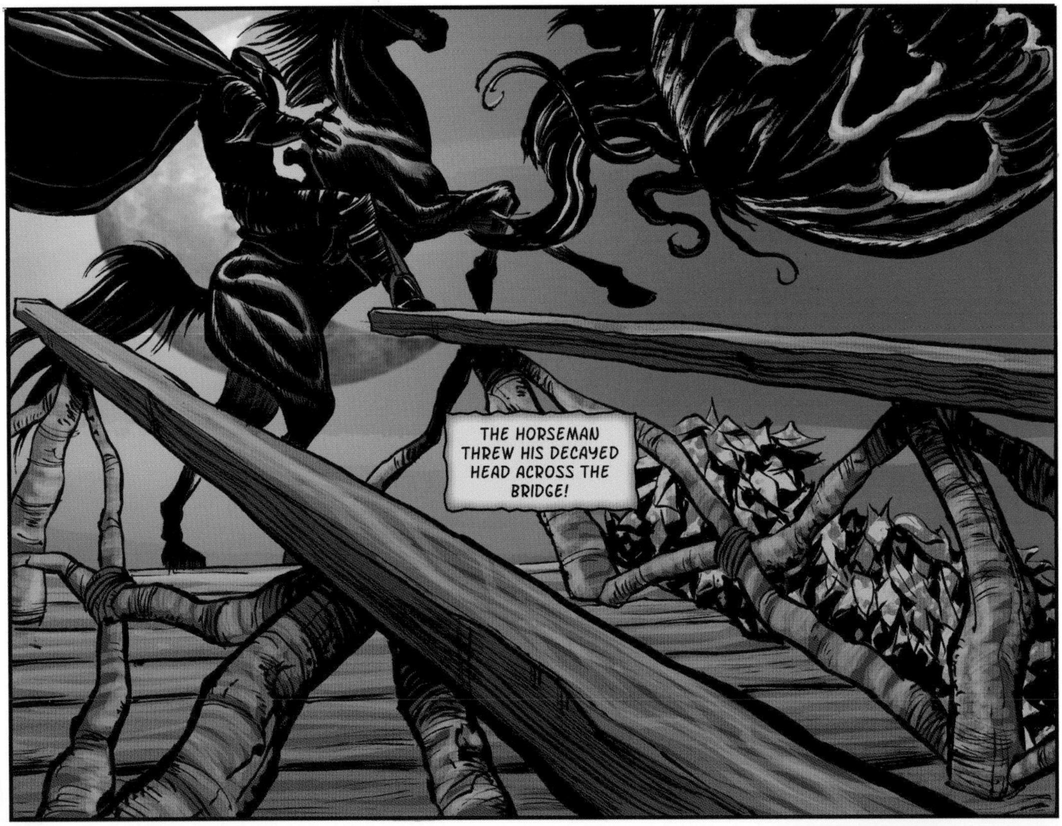
THE HORSEMAN THREW HIS DECAYED HEAD ACROSS THE BRIDGE!

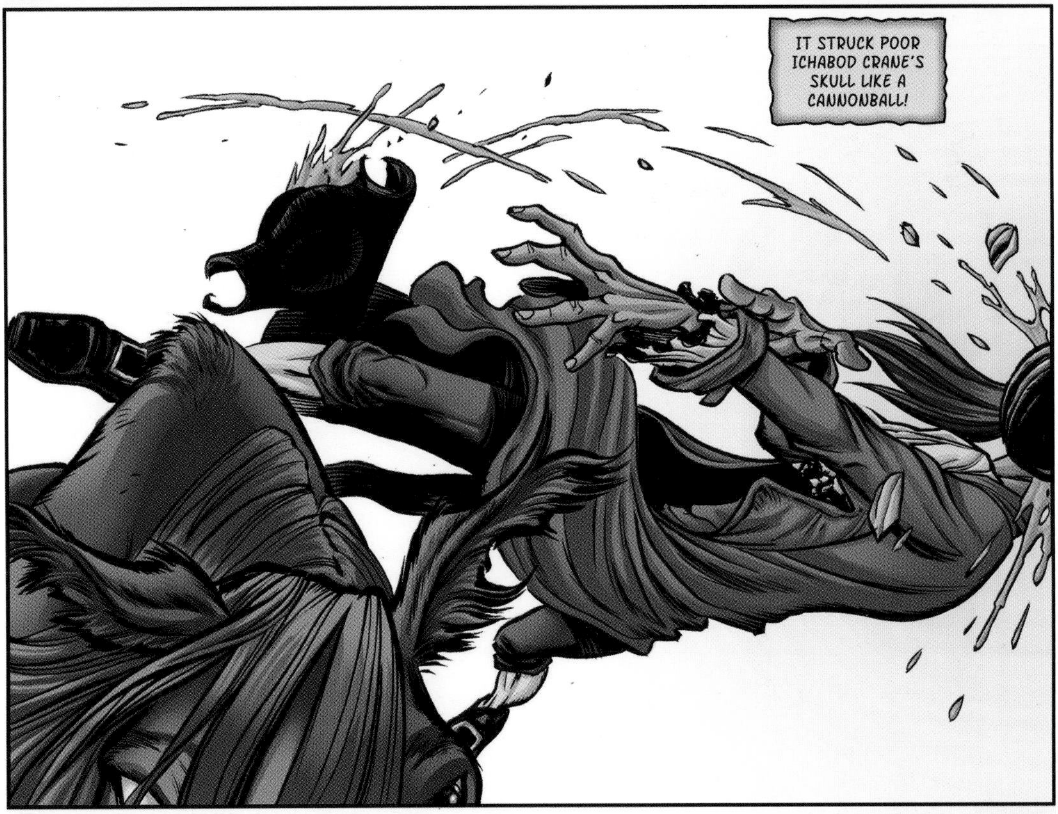
IT STRUCK POOR ICHABOD CRANE'S SKULL LIKE A CANNONBALL!

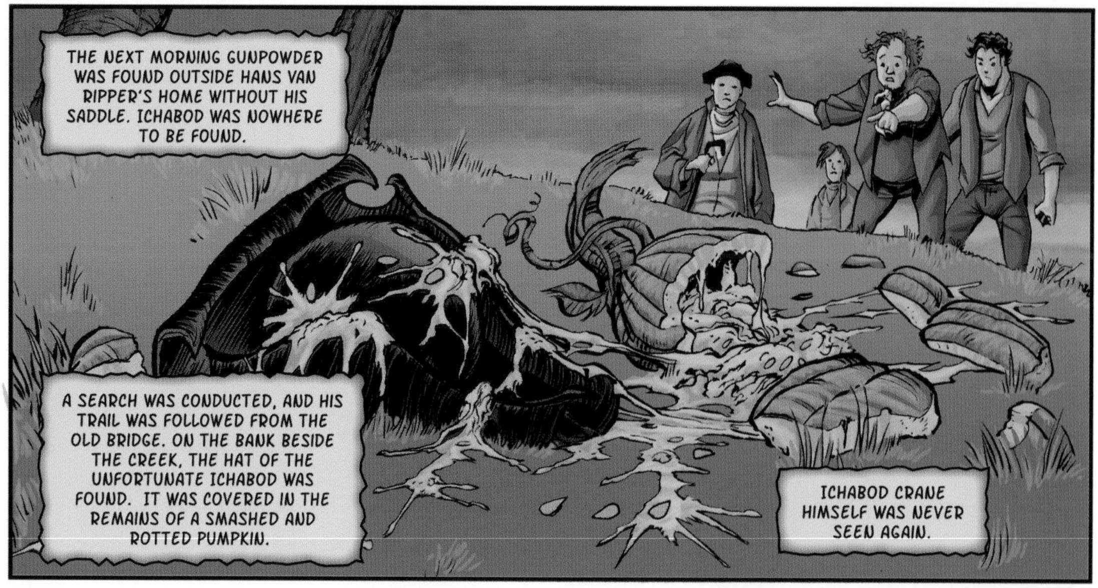
THE NEXT MORNING GUNPOWDER WAS FOUND OUTSIDE HANS VAN RIPPER'S HOME WITHOUT HIS SADDLE. ICHABOD WAS NOWHERE TO BE FOUND.
A SEARCH WAS CONDUCTED, AND HIS TRAIL WAS FOLLOWED FROM THE OLD BRIDGE. ON THE BANK BESIDE THE CREEK, THE HAT OF THE UNFORTUNATE ICHABOD WAS FOUND. IT WAS COVERED IN THE REMAINS OF A SMASHED AND ROTTED PUMPKIN.
ICHABOD CRANE HIMSELF WAS NEVER SEEN AGAIN.

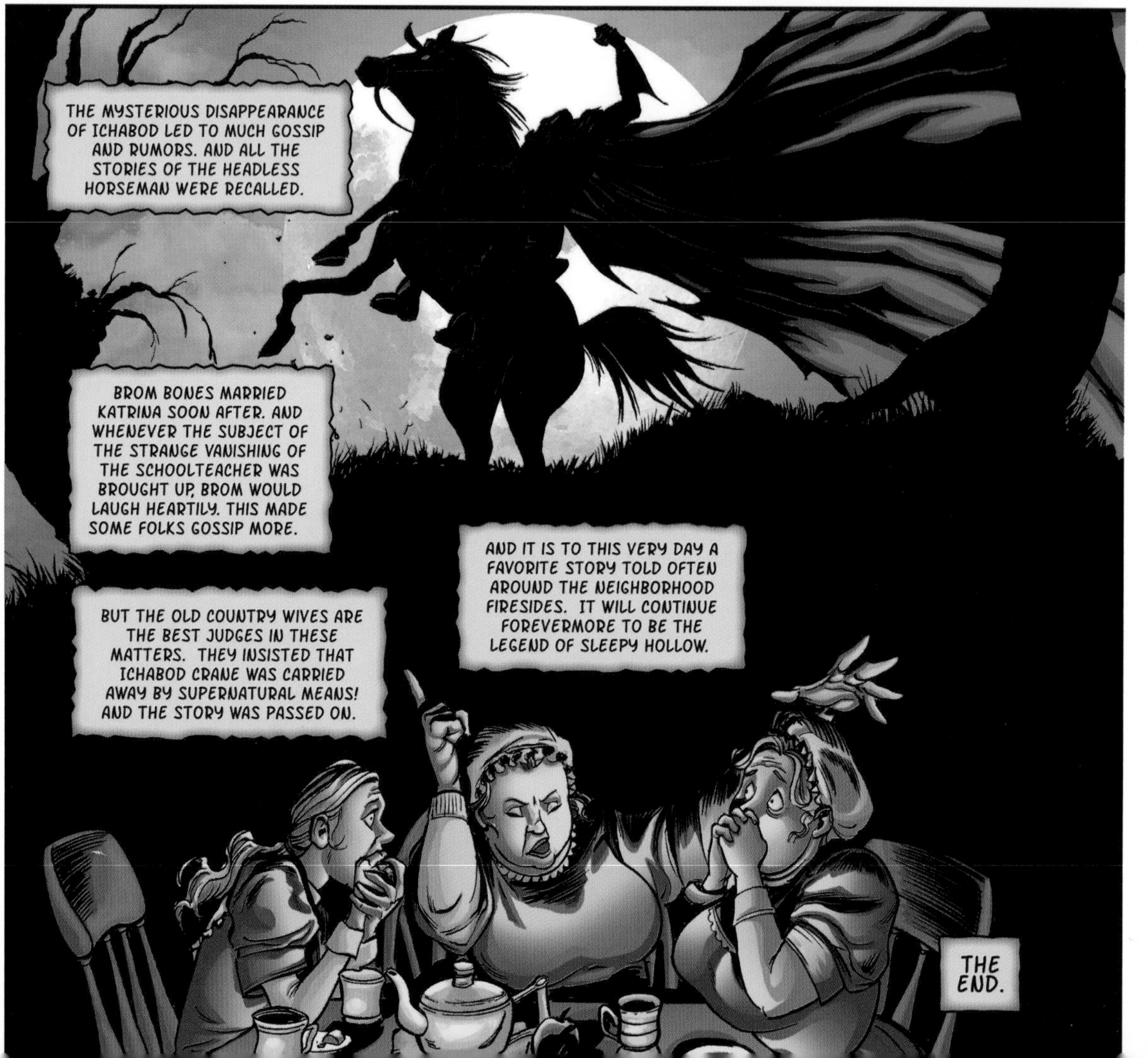
THE MYSTERIOUS DISAPPEARANCE OF ICHABOD LED TO MUCH GOSSIP AND RUMORS. AND ALL THE STORIES OF THE HEADLESS HORSEMAN WERE RECALLED.
BROM BONES MARRIED KATRINA SOON AFTER. AND WHENEVER THE SUBJECT OF THE STRANGE VANISHING OF THE SCHOOLTEACHER WAS BROUGHT UP, BROM WOULD LAUGH HEARTILY. THIS MADE SOME FOLKS GOSSIP MORE.
BUT THE OLD COUNTRY WIVES ARE THE BEST JUDGES IN THESE MATTERS. THEY INSISTED THAT ICHABOD CRANE WAS CARRIED AWAY BY SUPERNATURAL MEANS! AND THE STORY WAS PASSED ON.
AND IT IS TO THIS VERY DAY A FAVORITE STORY TOLD OFTEN AROUND THE NEIGHBORHOOD FIRESIDES. IT WILL CONTINUE FOREVERMORE TO BE THE LEGEND OF SLEEPY HOLLOW.
THE END.

# Washington Irving

Washington Irving was born on April 3, 1783, in New York City. He was the youngest of 11 children. Unlike his brothers, he did not have to attend college. Instead, Irving was apprenticed to a lawyer in 1801. But, he was soon bored.

The following year, Irving had his first story published in the *Morning Chronicle*. He took several trips up the Hudson River, into Canada, and throughout Europe.

In 1806, Irving returned home and passed the bar examination. However, he spent most of his time writing essays and stories with his brothers. In 1809, he completed the *Knickerbocker History of New York*.

During the next 10 years, Irving was an officer in the War of 1812 and worked several jobs in Europe. He never married. In 1819, he published *The Sketch Book of Geoffrey Crayon, Gent*. This collection of stories quickly became a success, especially the short stories in it called *Rip Van Winkle* and *The Legend of Sleepy Hollow*.

Due to the success of the *Sketch Book*, Irving was able to write full time. He returned to the United States in 1832 and continued to write. He died at home in Tarrytown, New York, on November 28, 1859.

## Irving Has Many Additional Works Including

Bracebridge Hall (1822)

The Alhambra (1832)

The Life and Voyages of Christopher Columbus (1828)

Astoria (1836)

Adventures of Captain Bonneville, U.S.A. (1837)

The Life of Oliver Goldsmith (1849)

Life of George Washington (1855-1859)

# Glossary

**bewitch** - to cast a spell over.

**dominant** - someone or something that has a stronger personality or presence than all others.

**erratic** - moving without a set direction or course.

**perplexity** - puzzlement.

**quest** - an act or journey to find something.

**reverie** - to be lost in thought.

**scepter** - a staff or baton used by a king or ruler.

**specter** - a ghost.

**trait** - a quality that distinguishes one person or group from another.

**unique** - being the only one of its kind.

**witching hour** - the time of night that is suitable for sorcery or supernatural events.

# Web Sites

To learn more about Washington Irving, visit ABDO Publishing Company on the World Wide Web at **www.abdopublishing.com.** Web sites about Irving are featured on our Book Links page. These links are routinely monitored and updated to provide the most current information available.